CONCIERGE AT THE DROWNED BABY INN

Christopher Hann

LVP
PUBLICATIONS

CONCIERGE AT THE DROWNED BABY INN

proclaimed Kiwi with the New Zealand citizenship,
albeit enslaved in what was supposed to be his
home country. Being told and made implicate that I was
and still am "an alien", I faced not of my
future, the reason for my return.

"Kiang won?" I enquired.

"Maibe," they answered.

"No, but when I believe they had enough sense
of counting about right then and there. They did
not mention a number; upon the silent and neutral
understanding that there would be no ...

DON JIRAL

Rather than being the moniker of an Italian mob
boss with a questionable heritage, the
aforementioned words are in fact, to my
comprehension at least, a commonly used
colloquialism in Korean for the phrase "money
bullshit". Don being money, and Jiral being bullshit.

And such was the nature of the summer job I
had taken at the Drowned Baby Inn (henceforth
D.B.I., for sake of some decency).

To add perspective, an act of Don Jiral connotes
spending in the form of lavish vanity and
wastefulness. Blowing through your TAB winnings
at night clubs with bottles of Dom Perignon (as if
our drunk nineteen-year-old tastebuds could discern
any difference) is Don Jiral. Blowing through your
international student university funds at the Skycity
Casino is just toxic addiction.

So hence I found myself back in the East Asian
Peninsula, broke and embarrassed, a self-

proclaimed Kiwi with no New Zealand citizenship, utterly displaced in what was supposed to be his home country. Being the stupid ingrate that I was (and still am, to an extent), I dared not tell my parents the reason for my return.

"Gap year." I explained.

"Huh." They answered.

Thinking back, I believe they had caught scent of something afoul right then and there. They did not interrogate further, upon the silent and mutual understanding that there would be no more support from them, financial or otherwise, for the rest of my adult life. The options were clear: make enough money to go back to New Zealand, or more realistically, wait for my conscription and join the godforsaken army. Either way, I needed a job.

One would be surprised at the sheer plethora of small, inhabitable islands that envelop the South Korean Peninsula. Consequently, many of them were being commercialized as get-away resorts: some open to the public, others much more discreet. As life sometimes transpires, a helping hand came by in the form of an acquaintance, whom I will call Matt.

A couple years my senior, Matt and I became friends by way of indulging in the usual vices, but it was our unbridled zeal for all things horror that solidified our camaraderie. Movies were an obvious. Horror Attractions were fun—but it was the kind of fun you had amongst a company of tipsy friends and, if luck would have you, a female companion clinging to your arm. (I did have a girlfriend at the time, but courtesy to my gambling problem the relationship soured quickly). Out of respect for all the talented actors that work in such establishments, I dare not label the experience as "cheap scares". However, at least for us horror enthused duo, such experiences were, well, fun. Not frightening. We drew up a map of all the famous attractions we wished to visit. The famed Hospital Ward in Yamanashi, Japan topped the list. We even considered the kidnap-torture gimmick they had going in the States, and in the end decided physical maltreatment was not our cup of tea—but the place remained on the list. Despite our grand plans for adventure, the obvious (and not so harsh) reality was that a fool and his money are soon parted, and Matt had to relocate to Korea. I followed suit a year later. By then these were all by-gone fantasies and I had already decided to let exciting memories be.

Matt explained over the phone why I fit the bill.

ONE: Candidate must come as a recommendation from a current employee.

TWO: Candidate must be able to commit, minimum six months.

THREE: Candidate must be of good health.

FOUR: Candidate must be willing to live on a remote island; and most importantly

FIVE: Candidate must not be easily spooked.

Island slave was the first thought I had.

Dragging off unsuspecting youngsters off on boats, working them as salt miners or crab fishers, trapped in a remote island with no police or Labor Department to speak of... Employment contract? What employment contract? Now move that rubble before we decide not to feed you! *Matt, are you trying to sell me off as an island slave?*

Then Matt dropped a name which hushed all my urban-myth-fueled worries. An heir, or a part heir to be exact, to a multinational conglomerate. The kind of conglomerate whose logo you might see three times in an afternoon. Due to the nature of Korean land laws, the heir could not find enough loopholes to privatize the island—but he sure as hell owned every building on it. And by every building, Matt really meant one. A private resort by the name of D.B.I. The premise had an accommodation license, a food and beverage license, and all other licenses required for running a hotel. In fact, it was Matt's older cousin ('Big Cuz', whom I later grew very fond of), a high-end chef working in D.B.I.'s kitchen, who had recommended him a job there. I was arriving at the imminent question: who in their sane mind would choose "Drowned Baby Inn" as a hotel's trading name?

Get this, said Matt. At a certain point during the night, the hotel turns into a...

Matt seemed to be searching for words.

"A haunted house?" I helped.

"Well, yes, a haunted house."

Matt seemed rather averse to using this term. Admittedly the place was a horror attraction; a commercial entity providing goods (by way of accommodation, food, and other amenities) and services (by way of "entertainment") in exchange for money. But he was quick to point out some other features that, in combination, stood out as a stark anomaly in comparison to other establishments of its ilk.

There were no actors involved.

Refreshing, I thought. My imagination quickly raced to animatronics, optical illusions, video effects, immersive auditory design and (in my childish hopes) the utilization of 'next generation' holograms. Screaming actors in clown costumes certainly had appeal, but for seasoned horror masochists such as Matt and myself, that appeal had turned stale some time ago. If the place was as well-kept as Matt described, I could be in for a good surprise.

The place had no set passages.

Meaning, the guests were let free to roam the premises in any fashion or trajectory they desired. I had heard of something similar to this—an "interactive play" where audiences were encouraged to explore a vast complex at their own pace, as actors in their designated spots performed various routines and postmodern dance numbers. Perhaps D.B.I. took on the recent fad of Room Escapes?

These were, in essence, puzzle solving exercises with a loose narrative to hold the experience together. At this point in our conversation, I had many bubbling questions for my friend, and was quite sold on the opportunity.

"There's only one guest per night." said Matt.

"Per room?"

"No, for the entire hotel."

I gave this a moment of thought.

"And how many rooms are there in D.B.I?"

Twenty-three, explained Matt, although only one of them was functional, being the actual room where the lone guest stayed in. The remaining twenty-two were part of the set piece. My lack of a degree in hotel management did not stop me from immediately questioning the math behind this operation. Without divulging into the details of the overheads and expenses, the establishment at maximum capacity could only entertain three hundred sixty-five guests in a given year. That could not be profitable.

Of course, when asked about the price of a night's stay at the D.B.I., matters of confidentiality barred Matt from answering forthrightly. Which in fact bars me now also, so if I may describe it in Matt's own words: about a quarter of an average man's annual salary.

"Wow," I said. "That sounds like Don Jiral."

I left for the island on the following Monday.

For the next part I will describe in brief detail what a typical guest might see on their way to the D.B.I.

The anecdotal guest, whom I will name Alfred, will arrive on the island at noon precisely. He would have been brought in a small but luxurious yacht, with fancy refreshments to match his pallet—this is an expensive vacation after all. The sturdy yet visibly old planks of the wooden dock lead to a flight of granite stairs, on top of which he will find a dark Bentley awaiting him, parked by the gravel road. It is here when Alfred must turn in his wallet, mobile phone, and any other personal or electronic devices in possession. He will not see these again until next morning.

There have been, of course, a few sneaky patrons who had miniature camcorders wired in their clothing. The management (no doubt by the orders of our wealthy proprietor) instructed us to pay no attention to this—the footage was likely to be blurred and incoherent, and the lack of any revelatory elements would only spice up the mystique.

Returning to Alfred, he must now make the first of his many choices on the island. Naturally, he is offered a ride on the Bentley towards the hotel using the main road. Or, if the weather is good (miraculously it always was), Alfred may prefer to make the journey on foot; a breezy, thirty-minute stroll across the beautiful meadows. Every single guest in my memory has chosen the walk.

A little trouble begins even before Alfred reaches the hotel.

No one had told him that there would be a fork in the trail. No one had lied, obviously, but the lack of mention of any diverging pathways had eliminated from his mind all thought of the possibility of getting lost.

'Silly,' he would think, as he instinctively feels for his phone and realizes he has given it away.

"I enjoy little details like this." I remember Mr. K telling me, our head concierge who oversaw staff training. "People aren't very deliberate when they reach for their phones. You feel a sudden rush of panic, and before that panic turns to frustration, you remember that it is in your backpack, safe and sound, and the panic turns into relief. It is sort of like that. Except you are alone on an island in the middle of nowhere."

To Alfred's left, the trail continues down the meadow, until it disappears into a dark, rather ominous looking tree line. To his right, not so far from him and in plain sight, lies a hedge maze.

Trite, one might think, as did I when I first heard of it. Hedge mazes, or just mazes in general, are a staple of horror attractions; in fact, the concept of escaping a labyrinth forms the foundation of many such establishments.

Except, no one asked for a maze *here*. In Alfred's case, the maze was never part of the deal. No one told him there would be a maze, he had not expected a maze, and he can see no blood-splattered panel at the entrance of the maze reading:

ENTER AT YOUR OWN PERIL!

In place of such conspicuous signage, there is a small but well-kept rose bush and a harmless enough statue of a cherub, which we keep a little mossy on purpose. The walls of the hedge itself is not truly a wall; it is a mass of tangled vines and flowers that bear little resemblance to the rigid green surface we are usually accustomed to.

Alfred is going to enter that maze. They all do. They simply paid too much money to miss out on any potential entertainment.

But for a tingle of claustrophobia (inherent to most mazes of this sort), there is nothing that catches Alfred's attention here - right until his seventh or eighth turn, depending on the direction he has taken. He encounters another cherub, not dissimilar to the one he just saw near the entrance. After a few more turns he finds another. Then another. This goes on just enough to plant the seeds in his mind that, perhaps, just maybe, he is going in circles.

Being a seasoned connoisseur of adventures such as this, Alfred catches the drift and grins.

The direction the angels are facing at each turn must lead to the exit—or to wherever the metaphoric Dungeon Master intends to lead him. A neat touch, thinks Alfred; a pleasant enough *amuse-bouche* to tonight's main course. The host of this island respects his sense of initiative and imagination, and in an industry where unilateral sensory bombardment is the standard, decisions such as this make for a nice introduction. As trite of a concept a hedge maze may be, Alfred finds himself quite enjoying this little mid-afternoon walk.

Then there's the ladder and the garden shears. Just lying discarded in the middle of the track. Despite the rust, the tools certainly aren't—or certainly don't seem to be—props.

According to Mr. K, the intended effect of this to arouse a mixture of reactions, ones that the guest themselves cannot place a finger on. The term 'uncanny valley' does not just pertain to visual perception, he explained. It can also apply to situations.

Alfred's first question: were these left here on purpose?

Should the answer be no, then the conclusion is simple. Either the gardener has forgotten to retrieve them by mistake, or perhaps worse, gardening is being carried out at this very moment. This isn't an impossible scenario: as a matter of fact, Alfred was never made aware of the existence of this maze and had entered at his own volition—so the precise timing of his arrival may not have been guessed. In any case, the finding causes Alfred some minor annoyance as he feels the 'illusion' of the experience breaking just a little.

Perhaps the gardener will appear around the corner, apologizing for the error and wishing him good luck.

But should the answer be yes? That just spawns more questions.

There are certain formulas that a self-proclaimed horror attraction is subject to, and most of them are brought in via expectations of the guests, predominantly through their past experiences at competing establishments. Perhaps what Alfred finds around the corner is not an actual gardener, but a howling scissor wielding maniac who chases him down the maze, Texas-Chainsaw-Massacre-style. Or perhaps it will be just a gardener. The important point is that Alfred does not know.

"Hello?" says Alfred, loud enough for anyone in the vicinity to hear him. (Variations of this include "Anybody around?" or "You forgot your ladder!" The merrier the call-out, the more anxious the guest.) The reason for this call-out is twofold: to (a) alert the real-life gardener that a guest is in the premises, or (b) announce to the professional actor at hand that he is ready for the oncoming challenge.

Of course, no one is in the vicinity.

If Alfred has a heart attack right now, it will be no less than two hours until his body is discovered. He is absolutely alone in these meadows, and the more Alfred progresses down the endless green aisle, the more inexplicably uncomfortable this notion becomes. Cherubs appear more abruptly around corners now, and Alfred finds himself jolting, just a little. Not because the statue startled him. But because he was expecting something, or someone, else.

There are no surprises here, maybe with the exception of a tiny pond at the clearing located at the center of the maze (The pond is very shallow: we can't afford a drowning incident and no one is around to help).

'Random,' Alfred thinks, as he finally arrives at the exit. Depending on how the night unfolds, he may be correct.

The trail now leads him to another entry into the gloomy tree line, which eventually meets up with the main road. It is a short while until Alfred reaches the D.B.I—or to be precise, what we call the Front-House Resort. The Resort contains all the amenities expected of a five-star hotel—a bar, swimming pool, sauna, a quaint but elegant dining hall—all fully staffed and all for Alfred alone. The Resort is where the guest may recoup some type of recompense for the extravagant amount of money he had spent for a night's stay on the island. Don Jiral is Don Jiral only when the splurger feels a sickly sense of satisfaction.

For Alfred's lunch, Big Cuz has prepared an appetizer of pan-seared scallops with yuzu dressing, a main course of Matsutake mushroom risotto finished with black truffle, and tiramisu for dessert.

As he chows down, Alfred reflects on the rather deflating and uneventful trip down the rose petaled labyrinth he had taken earlier.

"Excuse me. What's the deal with the maze?" he may ask.

"Maze?" we are trained to answer. "My apologies sir, we are not very familiar with the island outside of the premises."

At no point in time are we allowed to acknowledge the existence of the maze. I am certain there is some type of pseudo-psychology behind this, but never bothered to ask Mr. K.

And so, Alfred is left to meander for the remaining hours of sunlight.

We casually recommend him to pay a visit to the hill just on the side of the Resort, right around six p.m. The view of the sky is quite beautiful there, blazing orange and pink as darkness graciously swallows the surroundings, creeping over the meadows, creeping over the hill, until the shining windows of the D.B.I are the only source of light that survives on the island.

Dinner will be served at seven.

Check in is at nine.

In spite of the name value of the wealthy conglomerate that possessed this business, employee wages were, well, just wages. Pay rate for a trainee remained strictly at minimum, with a pennywise raise after a four-week training period, after which one was able to don the title: 'Concierge at the Drowned Baby Inn'. Staff turnover was surprisingly low however, and after some self-reflection I arrived at my own conclusions as to why this was the case.

Materially, the provision of staff meals (which were, to my personal standard, always excellent) and a free roof over my head spoke volumes in terms of benefits. Having blown through a small fortune once, I was at least able to come to grips with the very simple (yet often hazy) financial principle that controlling your expenditure is important for saving. The opportunity to earn without the ability to spend was very attractive to me at the time.

Then, of course, was my gambling.

The arbitrary 'cold-turkey' that the island served me was monumental in turning my habits around. Looking back, I imagine all of us were in need of some severance from the problems that plagued us on the mainland—all of us in need of some solid ice frozen turkey, whichever form it took. Many staff stayed on for as long as they could. And, tragically, some never left.

"Oof," said JY, when I explained to her the reason behind my presence on the island.

JY had joined the team around the same time as Matt, and I believe it was our bilingual natures that allowed us to gel so quickly. A former stage actor in Manhattan, troubles with the almighty U.S. Visa had left her searching for a job in her estranged home country—not so different from us Kiwi lads. My fondest memory of the trio include sweeping away the maple leaves on the aforementioned forest trail (a walk through which, despite my previous descriptions, can be quite romantic) and the occasional chatter over Soju on our mutual nights off. New Zealand lingo is hilarious to Americans apparently, and Matt and I were more than happy to divulge.

Being the less experienced of the two, my initial duties revolved around the Front House Resort.

I should make it clear that the Front House Resort and the D.B.I are two distinct entities. Any trainee, such was my case, would spend most days cleaning, mopping, folding, wiping, some more mopping, and occasionally smiling when approached by the guest during daylight hours. My lack of detailed description of the Resort is not wholly without purpose—imagine any modern high-end establishment and there you have it.

The Inn, on the other hand, is a contraption.

The two complexes are separated by way of a stone courtyard, only to be crossed once check-in time has arrived.

The style of the architecture, according to Mr. K, is that of 1930s Seoul (called 'Kyeong-Seong' at the time), an era of Japanese annexation over Korea, where the cultural residue of the two Asian nations, coupled with the aesthetics of Western urbanization all became muddled into a peculiar melting pot. The Inn is no doubt Western in its look (or 'classic' Western, though I cannot verify what this means exactly). The roofing of the terrace, however, is made of Giwa stone tiles (think East Asian castles), and the hallways are sparsely adorned with paper folding screens, portraying artwork. A touch overboard and the décor may collapse into what some critics may call "tacky orientalism"—but in my opinion the balance seemed perfect. Notwithstanding the mechanical ingenuity that powered the building, the building itself was something to behold—let alone explore.

This is where Alfred will be staying the night—but not before dinner.

Returning to our anecdotal guest, Big Cuz has prepared quite a show for his evening meal. Beluga caviar on a bed of Scottish salmon and Caprino cheese is served as the appetizer (a small glass of Grey Goose vodka accompanies this—but only a glass. Some liquid courage may be needed, but too much can dull the experience). Henceforth there is a salad with langoustine in a blood-orange marinade, Hanwoo beef and artichoke with wine jus, and fried sweetbreads on lard with, of course, ample amounts of truffle. Some nice enough sorbet is offered as dessert.

"The temptation is real," Big Cuz used to say, pondering whether he should just stay on the island forever. Having come from a competitive Michelin background, cooking for a single paying guest per night—no matter the complexity of the dishes—was little above child's play to his standard.

Alfred quite enjoys his dinner. What he enjoys more is a napkin that has mysteriously slipped on to his table during the course of the evening, with a bright-red kiss mark and a message written in lipstick: *Find me at the Seagull Lounge, tonight.*

'So it begins,' he gloats in anticipation.

Staff are allowed to react candidly to Alfred's comments in relation to this memo. Unlike the case with the hedge maze, there is a certain fun to be had when both the guest and the host 'are in' on the joke —this is entertainment, after all, and forcing a suspension of disbelief for too long can have the opposite of the desired effect.

Or so says Mr. K, our head concierge and also self-appointed chief psychologist.

"Is this from you?" Alfred asks me.

"No, sir," I answer, returning his grin in kind. "But it seems you have a secret admirer."

The clock hits eight-thirty and it's time to go over some housekeeping.

Most of these points have already been signed off at registration (please do not destroy the place, please tell us if you are ill, it's not our fault if you die, not liable, not liable, so on and so forth), so we keep things brief. Alfred is reminded that we have eyes on him at all times, with the exception of his guest room of course. Details are left vague. We dodge any questions in relation to the contents of the Inn itself.

Upon the moonlit courtyard, Alfred sees for the first time the structure that is the D.B.I. An iron gate guards its exterior, not dissimilar to a nineteenth century mental institution. The gate locks behind his back, with an audible *clunk.* Alfred is led swiftly to his room, given little chance to fully appreciate the décor and layout of the antique corridors. There is time, he reminds himself.

Politely yet assuredly, we usher him in.

> *Dear Guest,*
> *Welcome to Room 11.*
> [In accordance with the law and the ethics of sound business practice, we guarantee your privacy in this room. Please make yourself at home.
>
> As you are reading this, the door behind you has been locked electronically. It will unlock at some time between now and midnight. When this happens, you will know.
>
> There are no other guests in this building besides yourself, but should you happen to encounter someone please refrain from physical contact. There is an interphone on the table to the left side of your bed for any emergencies, but the line will no longer be operational the moment you decide to leave this room.

You are always welcome back here.]
Yours Truly,
Concierge at the Drowned Baby Inn.

There are several white lies in this conspicuous letter of welcome that Alfred finds on his mahogany desk. The interphone is always operational, but true to our word we do not pick it up. Upon multiple attempts (also depending on how far the guest has progressed), we manually turn the line to some heavy breathing.

Upon further attempts we playback to the guest a recording of what other guests had said over such calls. Genuine, real life recordings of paying guests in the past.

"Hello?" Alfred might say should he decide to call it quits.

"Hi."

"Oh—"

"Look, that was fun, it was great, but I'd like to return to the lobby now, please."

"What?"

"I can hear you fucking breathing, man."

Allow me to assure you: lest the business be caught in a lawsuit, there are definitely ways of quitting the D.B.I, which I will discuss in later parts. The interphone just isn't one of them.

After checking that the door has indeed been locked behind him, Alfred has around an hour to get comfortable with his immediate surroundings. The interior is what can be described as Victorian gothic, but not on the luxurious side. The bed side lamps are in the shape of bonsai pine trees, adding the Asiatic flare I had mentioned earlier. The carpet is a dreadful green, and with the exception of the bathroom (which we must allow for brightness to mitigate accidents), the overarching atmosphere is dark and gloomy.

Or dim and cozy, should one be partial to this type of appeal.

Returning to the mahogany desk, Alfred finds some books on the shelf. Picture books, actually, the kind meant for children aged five to ten, but unlike the rudimentary (or 'child-friendly') style of writing contained within the pages, the illustrations therein cannot be labelled as such.

Below are summaries of the ones I remember.

THE FOX SISTER

[Long ago there lived a family whose members consisted of a father, a mother, a brother old, and a brother young. Both the patriarch and matriarch of this small clan wished for a daughter as their third child, but as old age would have it, bearing a child at all seemed far out of reach.

"Pray at the fox shrine!" advised a shaman, an old wretch. "Pray with your heart!"

And so they did, and so they were begotten a baby girl, their precious baby girl, who grew up with a firm monopoly on the couple's unbridled love. But from her seventh birthday, the family cattle began to perish. Every night, one by one.

The firstborn, the eldest son, was summoned at his father's behest. With a pitchfork he kept careful watch over the livestock at night, and what he saw terrified him.

His sister, his seven-year-old sister, crept into the barn and sat behind the cattle. Her left hand grew claws the size of scythes, as she plunged them into the rear-end of one of the poor animals, thereafter ripping out its heart and liver, and proceeded to devour them greedily.

"You jealous fool!" screamed the father upon

hearing the firstborn's honest accounts, and banished him far, far away.

The cattle kept perishing, and it was now the second son's duty to keep watch.

He, however, fearing the fate that had befallen his older brother, lied.

Three years passed until the firstborn returned home out of famine and hunger. The family farm had been desolated, with no one to be seen except his little sister.

"Where is father?" The firstborn asked.

"He is well." She answered.

"Where is mother?"

"She is well." She answered, yet again.

"Where is my younger brother?"

She did not bother answering this time and descended upon him with her claws withdrawn. She ripped him to pieces and consumed his flesh, just like she did with the rest of his family.]

THE MONK, THE CUCUMBER AND THE LADY FAIR

["What use is beauty in a wife who is fruitless without child!"

Complained the husband, an heir apparent to a noble family. These were difficult times for Lady Fair, who, despite the first few joyful years of marriage, now faced blatant scorn for her alleged infertility. Her husband was an heir after all, and in the grand scheme of succession, having an heir to an heir seemed vitally important.

Rumors, as they often do, spread like algae on a pond, and it soon arrived at Lady Fair's ears that her husband intended to cast her out, in search for a new, child-yielding wife.

Being devout of faith, Lady Fair prayed daily at the temple upon the mountain.

The monk who resided on the temple grounds heard of her troubles, and decided to help out of kindness of heart.

"Consume this," said the monk, handing over an ice-cold cucumber that grew in misty valley of the mountain. "Consume this, and thou shall be with child."

And miraculously this was true. Her happiness was short lived, however, as her husband was a skeptic of all things mystic.

Rumors, as they often do, spread like algae on a pond, and it soon arrived at the husband's ears that the so-called cucumber was but a crass euphemism for something else, hinting at a sordid relationship between the monk and his wife.

After a glass of rice wine, skepticism turned to rage, and after ten glasses more, rage turned to fury. And on that fateful and drunken night he strangled Lady Fair, murdering her and the fetus that grew in her womb. His fury unrelented, he picked up an axe and marched up the mountain.

"How will your magic help you now?" he asked, as he buried the axe deep into the monk's skull.

To further desecrate the carcass, he withdrew a knife and ripped open the monk's robes—only to discover that there was no work to be done.

The monk, unbeknownst to him, had been a woman.

Confused, the husband wandered the mountainside for the remainder of the night. And when the sun rose on the horizon, he found a suitable location and hung himself from a pine tree.]

To clarify, these stories are all based on existing folklore, though their renditions at the D.B.I are no doubt much more graphic. There are many other materials strewn around Room Eleven to help Alfred pass the time—some are storybooks like the above, but others appear much more random, such as a Da Vinci-esque sketch of a man's head with the ears and eyes sawn shut. I will discuss these materials in more detail as they become relevant.

Chime bells of a grandfather clock ring throughout the hallway: an unmistakable prompt that the door of Room Eleven has now been unlocked.

This is a little sooner than Alfred expected; midnight is the symbolic threshold to mark the start of a game and, even without a watch on his wrist, Alfred knows it can't be midnight just yet. He may choose to linger in his haven, lest he wants to revisit some of those pleasant tales to keep in his memory, or wants to search under every crack for hidden secrets (such is not the case; we prefer to keep the guest room as unturned as possible). Eventually he will depart from Room Eleven, knowing that once he does, even the false sense of security that the interphone provides will be gone, leaving him quite alone to explore this vast complex.

He opens the door and finds it is pitch black.

Due to the nonlinear design of a guest's potential

trajectory through the D.B.I, it is difficult from hereon to describe events chronologically. There are, of course, what we call 'main attractions' that form the central route of the journey throughout the premises (the lipstick memo being related to one of them). These invariably entail some sort of complex engineering or require a high budget to maintain—so despite the ever-deep pockets of our Inn's proprietor, replacing such attractions would not be ideal.

Side attractions, on the other hand, underwent routine updates, both in terms of look and the related narrative (I am not aware of any return customers to date, but word of mouth travels and there was a need to keep some aspects of the business fresh).

Whereas main attractions were staged in the common areas of the D.B.I (such as the aforementioned Seagull Lounge), side attractions were predominantly based on the guest rooms, so the customer usually experienced these first. In my personal honesty, there weren't too much ingenuity involved in the recycling of these minor exercises, as the repertoire was quite formulaic:

(a) The customer encounters something in room X;

(b) The said something leads the customer to room Y, where they will discover something else   that provides further insight into the events of room X;

    (c) Upon the customer deciding to return to room X, something will have changed drastically.

The art of the side attraction lay in its execution more so than on its design. It was absolutely critical that we did not ruin the experience by running into the guest by accident or leaving traces of inorganic manhandling. In this regard, the structural configuration of the D.B.I helped to serve our purpose.

Foremost, we had full discretion of when to lock or unlock any of the room doors from a control center located on the upper level of the D.B.I, inaccessible to the guest (to clarify, "full discretion" means discretion according to the manual). In this way, we could ensure that room Y is never unlocked before room X, so that the narrative integrity of the side attraction remains intact. Then again, it is the guest's own prerogative whether they want to indulge in each and every one of these distractions.

Naturally, rooms X and Y must be kept at a distance. Our eye in the sky (which had visibility in the dark) kept close track of exactly where the guest was maneuvering, and we had very tight windows of time to implement the required changes. We delivered these via drop-down attic doors located in every guest room (except of course, Room Eleven), which in turn is connected to the control center. The seemingly random bursts of chime bells in the halls are often used to mask what little ruckus we may make during this duty.

As one may appreciate, there is a reason why new employees were not allowed anywhere near the D.B.I during live operation.

Below are two of the various side attractions that I was involved in managing, but due to constant adjustments I must admit the details are foggy. As intriguing as I found them at first, the following account in particular has stuck with me for a different reason altogether.

THE MAN IN ROOM THREE

Room Three is locked during the initial stages of the night, although it is uncommon that a guest might ponder in that direction without actively searching for it.

What sets off the events is their entry into Room Fifteen.

The room belongs to a teenage boy, indicated by a pair of shoes, socks, a leather school bag with books (appropriate to the time period) and various articles of clothing in the wardrobe. The diary on his desk gives some insight into his origin, and though we played around with his backstory on multiple occasions, the overarching theme was that he arrived on this island with his parents—only to have them leave for the mainland the day after, promising swift return. They never did, and the boy was left abandoned in the D.B.I.

Ever since, he has been terrified of the man who resides in Room Three.

He knocks on his door every night, feigning the voice of his father. But behind the gentle coaxing of his words there is an insistent clinking of scissors, the metal shards of the rusty blade rasping maniacally against one another as the imposter demands entry. The man hides away in his room during daylight hours. He comes at night, only at night.

Should the guest now turn their mind to exploring Room Three, they will find its door aptly unlocked. A jump scare may be due upon entry, but in the D.B.I such instances are rare.

What the guest finds instead are suitcases, a lab coat by the bench, and a plethora of medical journals piled on the desk. One such journal is personal, and it reveals as follows:

The resident of this room (a doctor, by all accounts) arrived on the island with his son on a mission to cure him of Prosopagnosia. A neurological disorder that affects the brain's ability to recognize faces, the boy's condition had gotten to a point where he began to deny his own identity, debilitating him of any capacity to function in a normal, social world. The man wasn't staying in Room Three out of his own volition. His son had driven him out.

So there is a conundrum here, although most of the guest's questions appear to have been explained via the two contrasting journals. A family drama—a tragic one at that, and the somberness of the account seems to sit well with the mood of this dim establishment. If, however, one were to flip to the very end of the man's journal, written on the corner of the page is a red scribble that reads:

Need to get past the salt barrier. Need to fool child, and cut him.

Those of you who are familiar with East Asian shamanism (or just shamanism in general) may see where this is going.

The more vigilant of patrons would have noticed the thick lining of salt underneath the door when entering Room Fifteen. The very act of opening it, whether deliberated or not, would have scattered this lining—inadvertently breaking the barricade between the boy and whatever being he was trying to keep out.

This is not the only clue in relation to the man in Room Three, and it matters not if these are discovered in retrospect. There is a small, antique cupboard located along the corridors containing a 'to-do' list for the Inn's staff. The daily tasks and duties seem rather mundane, but for a single memo on the bottom of the page: "*To whoever keeps unlocking the door to Room 3: STOP*".

There are many bits of information such as the above, scattered around all corners of the D.B.I. When viewed in relation to one another, they eventually lead to some tentative conclusions:

  (a) there is no such thing as a man in
    Room Three,
  (b) Room Three has been out of use for
    many years, and
  (c) any person who claims to reside in

Room Three is not really a person.

We turn on the screaming when the guest exits the room. It resonates from Room Fifteen, just loud enough to be carried along the hallways.

Unlike surveillance cameras, where perfect concealment was difficult due to the control center requiring vision, auditory speakers could be easily hidden inside fake ventilation, and many such devices were installed strategically along the infrastructure.

We cut off the screaming abruptly when the guest, once again, approaches the boy's room. What they find inside is quite the artwork, if one could consider it such.

Made of silicone and gelatin, the boy sits in his chair. In place of where his head should be there are about a dozen surgical scissors, stuck forcefully into what remains of his trachea and windpipe. An elegant touch here is the blood—not the look and consistency of it, which is replicated easily enough, but the aroma.

Bottles of Rosé wine are left open to aerate in the sunlight. With a pinch of salt and a small touch of vinegar, one can reproduce a gentle yet distinct scent of blood—the kind you might taste when accidentally biting down on your own tongue. No doubt there are more powerful ways to replicate this; however, on the extreme off chance that a guest ingests some of the concoction, we had to ensure that the mixture was in no way toxic (this is a hypothetical—no guest was insane enough to try it).

Room Fifteen will be locked when the guest is done appreciating the extravaganza. Although, all throughout the night, they will be able to hear a merry whistling coming from beyond the door, with the unmistakable sound of scissors softly cutting through flesh—as if a piece of origami is being created with what remains of the boy.

"May I meet the gentleman?"

The question was posed by a female guest, who had an hour ago forfeited the remainder of her night in the D.B.I. I will name her Catherine, and unlike our anecdotal friend, this was a real existing customer.

As previously mentioned, there are guaranteed ways of quitting the experience outside of the interphone, one of which includes shouting desperately at the surveillance camera for a prolonged length of time. Catherine did not make it past the Seagull Lounge, and though visibly distraught initially, an offer of whiskey back at the Resort seemed to cheer her up rather fast.

Matt, JY and myself kept her company at the bar, as the presence of others is often desired after a time of isolation in the Inn, however short. If requested, we are encouraged to join the guest (though, only for a single glass), and I vaguely remember enjoying this candid conversation, the three of us no longer bound by any theatrical pretense.

Catherine's isolation, however, was not apparently absolute. She praised in great detail the acting abilities of the man in Room Three, an extremely senile gentleman (noted Catherine, worrying for his health) who was able to maintain the mirage behind his story without needless overacting. She had not expected a live actor (as word of mouth travels), but rather than upsetting the sense of immersion, his imposing yet soothing presence drew her further into the narrative.

"What the hell are you talking about?" I almost blurted out, but JY tugged at my sleeve just in time.

Matt simply smiled, thanked her for her compliments, and said he would pass them on to the actor.

"I'm afraid," he added, "that it might be difficult to meet him in person."

Needless to say, I questioned my colleagues after Catherine had departed, and what they explained to me was thus.

This was not the first time where a guest sighted an actor within Room Three. As a matter of fact, it happened every so often.

"Check the footage."

Of course, we did. Catherine, as with the other past guests who had entered Room Three, located the journal (as we had intended) and perused it. Then, after examining some of the furniture, she left. So the encounter with an actor was an obvious lie, and even if one were to be open-minded towards supernatural phenomena, we had physical proof that evidenced otherwise.

What irked me about this fabricated story was the proud blatantness of it.

The guests are more than aware of our omni-sight: our ever present 'eyes in the sky'. In fact (unless there are some immediate features that draw their attention), the surveillance camera is among the very first things that they look for when entering new territory—Room Three being no exception.

Our only plausible rationalization was that Catherine wanted to pull our legs, a metaphorical middle-finger towards the creators of this labyrinth, leaving its staff something spooky to dream about. As for the commonality of the story, perhaps there existed a secret circle of past and would-be guests, who corroborated on the narrative to add further weight to their lie.

The only folly to this theory was the guests' clumsy execution of it. If Catherine had sat on the bed and gazed into thin air for at least a minute, then yes, perhaps we might have been spooked. The lack of such performance, however, left us all scratching our heads about what exactly she wanted to achieve by mentioning this self-imagined actor.

As for the side attraction that was The Man in Room Three, management decided to replace it a week after Catherine's visit.

THE LONG STAYING PATRON

The inspiration for this attraction was discovered due to good fortune, on an evening where Matt and I were let free due to a guest's cancellation.

I, for the most part of the day, was helping Big Cuz with cooking the staff meals (to be clear: the preparation of *guest* meals was in the absolute control of our star chef—staff meals, on the other hand, always welcomed a helping hand). Whether for patrons or for employees, Big Cuz maintained his standards in the kitchen with an iron fist, and it is here where I took on board the very basics of hygiene, safety, storage, and preparation of food: an area of work where I was growing a rapid interest in.

We looked down upon the fresh lobster, langoustines, and the Dungeness Crab that lay on the bench before us. Being festive season in Korea, there were no guests booked for at least a few more days, by which time these beautiful crustaceans would have turned to frozen waste.

I looked at Big Cuz and raised an eyebrow.

"Hey, don't look at me," he said. "Go ask Mr.

K."

And with Mr. K's blessing, the staff were treated with the most luxurious rendition of spicy-seafood hot pot that I had personally ever tasted. After this jovial meal, Matt approached me with a piece of paper in hand.

"Check this out."

JY, being her official day off, had been working on some sketches during most of the afternoon. Her artistic predisposition extended beyond her love for theatre, and though she was rather shy to bring the notion forward, she had always hoped to contribute towards the creative side of the D.B.I.

It was a drawing of a man's head with the ears and eyes sawn shut—a draft version of what eventually became the Da Vinci-esque sketch located in Room Eleven.

"Pretty good," I remarked.

"Pretty good?" Matt retorted, clearly astounded by the quality of the work. "We've got to show this to Mr. K."

The stars seemed to align on this specific occasion, as upper management was requesting a new side attraction that involved more guest interaction with a humanoid animatronic. This was met by protest from the engineers (who did not reside on the island, often leaving it to Mr. K to voice their opinions), pointing out the logistical difficulties in maintaining such devices whilst guaranteeing the safety of both the guest and the attraction.

There were, of course, pre-existing animatronics at the D.B.I—but microscopic care had been exercised in ensuring their proper function, and biting off more than one can chew would likely lead to technical disaster.

A consensus was reached: a new animatronic will be introduced, but physical interaction would be restricted. This idea, however, presented a hurdle of its own. Without the use of an actor, any 'interaction' (or exposition, to be exact) would inevitably be unilateral in nature: a fancy stand-in for an information dump, or a mere cog in solving a puzzle—and the Inn had plenty of both already. Upper management, as is often the case, was hard set in pushing its agenda, and were now demanding a workable brief.

Stuck in between two stubborn oppositions, Mr. K had to suggest some type of compromise—and when presented with JY's sketch, a thread of a potential solution popped into his mind.

And thus was born the concept of The Long Staying Patron.

Room Thirteen, where the Patron resides, is a prison.

Upon opening the door, the guest will encounter a second door, made of steel, with a barred window that grants limited vision into the room's dark interior—the dim light from the corridors being the only source of illumination. There on the bed lies the Patron, his face just as grotesque as JY imagined, the gentle rising and falling of his blanket indicating life. Or a half-life, being the state that he is in.

Upon discovery he will tilt his head towards the door, but only slightly. The guest is left to gaze at him through the iron bars, perhaps hoping for another reaction, but none will be given in this first encounter. In this sense, the Patron's physical predicament turned out to be a stroke of brilliance: one may shout, jeer, laugh, or scream at a blind and deaf man all they like—but eliciting a response would naturally be futile.

Should the guest revisit Room Thirteen, they will find themselves face to face with the Patron, the leathery decay of his skin now much in plain view.

"Itchy."

He says, seemingly aware of the presence beyond the steel door.

"Left ear."

As with most attractions at the D.B.I, it is up to the guest's sole prerogative whether to oblige the Patron's indirect request. The space in between the bars is just wide enough to put one's fingers through —and good few seconds of caressing his ear will elicit a well-deserved:

"Oh!"

(Our motto is not to rely on jump scares, but then again, some are necessary.)

"You're a good boy."

Or girl, says the Patron, depending on the guest. Having completed this little task marks the end of the second encounter, but from the third, the guest may learn more about this poor man's namesake.

The Patron is out of sight now, although the sound of his breathing indicates he is leaning right next to the prison door.

"Don't trust the caviar."

He warns, and through disjointed sentences, tells the tale of his time at the D.B.I.

The Patron was brought upon the island by a very wealthy acquaintance, via a private invitation. An old motel was being renovated into what would be a luxury resort, and as a friend and business partner, he was one of the very first to experience the premises—free of charge. After a few nights' stay, the Patron was cordially encouraged to give any feedback on the commercial viability of the business.

Regrettably, the Patron found himself thoroughly unimpressed.

He laughed at the wealthy proprietor, mocking him for his irresponsible waste of money. The carpet was drabby, the décor was tasteless, and the lunacy that was the design of the Seagull Lounge was more than idiotic.

He did, however, enjoy the caviar he was served, the sole redeeming point of this failure of an establishment.

"The caviar, so creamy. So salty like finger-limes."

Having been humiliated in front of his staff, the proprietor sought to redeem himself, offering a full month of free accommodation for the Patron, whilst he took on the harsh feedback and worked on improvements. The Patron had no reason to accept —but for that sweet, salty taste of caviar that beckoned seductively at his tastebuds. The provision of the delicacy was his only condition, and the Patron would stay for long as he was required.

All that was thirty-six years ago.

"The caviar, it makes me itch. My ears, my eyes."

The Patron begins to lament.

"The caviar makes my eyes so itchy. It makes my throat dry, so I need to have some more. So salty like finger-limes, so salt-"

He stops, as if something is caught in his nostril.

"Need to sneeze, need to… eh… eh…"

A pause.

"Achoo!"

There is an ear-piercing *splat* as a monstrous amount of tiny black beads, mixed with viscous pink brain-matter go flying in every direction. And then silence.

The guest, of course, should be well protected behind the steel door. As the animatronic's physical appearance cannot be seen from the angle, we were able to utilize a rather simple yet potent pressure pump to decorate the finale of our Long Staying Patron.

From the guest's perspective at least, his head

had literally exploded from too much caviar.

We were in the middle of 'fly catching' when JY broke the news.

'Fly catching' was as straightforward as it sounds: we leave any type of pungent food waste in an insect-screen basket and simply close off the lid when enough had been caught. The tricky part was delivering these pests into the required containers used in the 'Kitchen' (capitalized, to differentiate from our actual kitchen where Big Cuz did the cooking). We looked up, swiping away at the insistent buzzing in our ears.

"I'm going away for a week," she said.

Her contribution to the success of the latest side attraction had earned her a few days of full paid leave, and coupled with her mother's upcoming birthday, the opportunity for a short vacation was well due.

Judging by his reaction, it was clear to me that Matt had known this ahead of time. It was also clear to me, as it might have been to any staff member who was attentive enough, that a mutual fondness had developed between the two.

"Here," she had whispered, as she discreetly passed the coveted lobster claw on to Matt's plate, the night of our spicy-seafood hot pot (a lobster only has two claws obviously, so whoever ended up with the prize would be considered lucky).

Ever being the gentleman, Matt declined, offering it back to her.

"I already had one," she responded nonchalantly.

'Liar,' I thought to myself with a cheeky grin.

Big Cuz and I had already consumed the other claw back in the kitchen, as a secret pat-on-the-back for a meal well prepared. Although blossoming relationships were quite against workplace policy, I believe everyone at the time (even Mr. K, who turned a blind eye) thought well of this rather endearing couple.

The week during JY's absence showcased the most productive version of Matt I had ever seen. Notwithstanding his normal course of duties, Matt embarked on a mission of self-development, beginning with an hour run every morning (which I was begrudgingly dragged along to). Knowing that his time on the island could not last forever, he began seriously planning his next step in life. Matt, unlike myself, was a bona-fide Kiwi with New Zealand citizenship, meaning that conscription was exempt, and a career was ahead. He would start by applying as an English tutor to make ends meet (he held a law degree after all, though he couldn't imagine himself in the profession), and from there he would gradually expand his vision to something more permanent. Thanks to his time at the D.B.I, his yearn for adventure, which had subconsciously obstructed him from working in the 'real world', had been largely fulfilled. He was ready to start building a more stable type of livelihood, one that could provide for not only himself, but others that he cared about.

A week and three days passed and there was no sign of JY.

Messages were unanswered. Calls rang cold.

When two weeks had gone by, Matt was seriously beginning to get nervous. He wanted to check on her well-being, but having come from different sides of the planet, we had no mutual acquaintances to link us through.

"She did a runner," conjectured one of the staff.

This was a conjecture, not a statement of fact. But the words seemed to stab deeply at the back of Matt's mind.

'Runners', as rare as they were, did happen. Foregoing any of the required procedures for resignation (such as giving a two weeks' notice, endeavoring to find a replacement, etc.), a runner would simply cut off all contact upon arrival on the mainland. I assume the sheer distance in space made this easier, at least in comparison to other jobs. With the sea in between oneself and the workplace, the decision to abandon all responsibility could be arrived at more comfortably.

"It broke the illusion," Matt kept repeating, much to the concern of both Big Cuz and I.

It was the confinement of the island, according to Matt, that gelled their mutual attraction—not genuine intimacy. The mere circumstance of having to rely on one another formed the foundation of their relationship, and when JY spent a week in normal society, she realized how fleeting this foundation truly was.

"She went back to the real world," he said.

"Mate, we are in the real world," I would have argued, but what Matt needed at the time was consolation, not reprimand. Eventually he accepted the situation and wished her well, though he would have deeply appreciated some closure from JY, as painful as it might have been.

Matt continued his morning runs, but no longer invited me along.

As experience would have it, he was quickly becoming one of the more senior of Concierges, always immaculate with his duties and praised for his work ethic—although his plans for the mainland seemed to be on halt.

He was still well liked by all of the staff, but we could not help but notice his growing dark circles, spreading ever so incrementally under the gloom of his gaze.

'This is a mistake.'

Thinks Alfred, staring into darkness.

Upon registration for a night's stay at the D.B.I, challenge was what Alfred had hoped for: the kind that tests his sense of intuition as well as his threshold for fear. Wading through these corridors in pitch black darkness, however, seems an impossibility—and having just embarked on his tour of the Inn, Alfred finds himself utterly stumped.

'This is a mistake. They forgot to give me a flashlight.'

It is here where Alfred must once again use his initiative, much like he did earlier in the hedge maze with the Cherubs.

The doors of all the guest rooms in the D.B.I, much like the doors of many commercial inns, are of heavy material that gently close on their own when left unattended. His only source of illumination, at least in the present moment, stems from Room Eleven—though it does little to lift the veil of shadow that drapes the cavernous hallways. All he can make out to either side of him is a sea of black, and as it becomes clear that Room Eleven is all the light he is going to get, Alfred arrives at a simple conclusion.

'I just have to find another room.'

Lest he be locked out in the dark, Alfred tests his room door from within. Seven seconds. Seven seconds of partial vision until the door becomes fully closed, after which he will be completely blind. Having satisfied himself that this is the only way, he places a hand on the wall of the corridor and takes his symbolic first step.

He decides to go right.

And a Right-Turn is what we internally call the Wrong-Turn, for with the exception of Room Ten (which itself is unilluminated), all subsequent doors remain locked for the time being. The preference to turn right is in part by design: from the point of view of a guest leaving Room Eleven, the exit swings open to the left. This means that the seven seconds of precious light can be best taken advantage of by going right, and naturally most guests tended to take this route, before tiring of their futile journey through the dark and deciding to return to home base.

Forced to take cautious steps, it takes Alfred no less than a minute to reach Room Ten, located just around the first corner.

Room Ten is what we call the 'Shushing Room', for upon making entry Alfred will hear a sharp and distinct:

"Shhhh!"

He feels around for a switch, but no cigar. The sole arbiter of light in this building is the control center, and until his run in with the Bell Boy, Alfred has no choice but to wander the corridors blinded.

The Shushing Room, admittedly, was an afterthought—chosen as a quick replacement when a minor side attraction went out of order. It was our management's firm belief that all twenty-three rooms of the Inn should be explorable at some point in time—any contrary to this mandate would amount to cheating the guests and their hard-earned money. Every single room were to be utilized, no matter the simplicity of the concept contained therein.

Should the guest, having eventually illuminated the premises, decide to return to Room Ten, they will find the walls adorned with seven paintings of seven children, all underwater with a finger over their lips (in the aforementioned *"Shhh!"* motion).

The children, as revealed by an art- magazine located in Room Twenty, belonged to the Inn's field keeper by the name of Ahn the Gardner. In a cottage located on a remote corner of the island, Ahn led a quiet life with his wife and seven offspring. The quiet life turned to one of silence, however, when his wife drowned in a boating incident one stormy afternoon. Ever since, Ahn was encapsulated by a rather odd belief: if he and his family were to keep a 'Vow of Silence' for a hundred consecutive days, his deceased wife would return to him reincarnated. Despite the strange nature of this vow, the children kept to it under their father's strict regime. But on day ninety-nine, the youngest suffered from a nightmare and awoke screaming, much to the dismay of Ahn. No one knows the exact details of the proceeding events that unfolded, but on the same day Ahn drowned all seven of his children and turned himself in to the authorities.

Ahn was committed to a mental asylum for twenty years, and it was during this period when he produced the paintings of his children. After his release he returned to the island and retook his job as the field keeper, tending to his rose gardens in the meadow in his spare time. He still keeps his vow, however, in firm belief that his days of silence will eventually bring his family back to him.

But I digress.

It's been some time since Alfred has been fumbling through the dark in futile search for an open room, and it occurs to him that he probably took a wrong turn at the starting point. And on his way back he meets the Bell Boy, or what echoes remain of him, though Alfred does not yet know the identity of whom they belong to.

Footsteps approach rapidly from the other end of the corridor.

Alfred freezes, readying himself for what may be the first true scare of the experience he signed up for. This is it—this is how it begins, he thinks. He knew that the host wouldn't miss out on an opportunity like this—a perfect target, vulnerable in the dark.

He expects the footsteps to stop right in front of him.

Will it scream? Will it pounce?

Or perhaps it will slink away in silence, leaving him with even more anxiety as he trudges on in blindness.

What Alfred doesn't expect is the footsteps to run right past him—or *through* him, to be exact. The width of the corridor means that if someone were to be approaching him directly—at a fast pace no less—they should have certainly made some physical contact, but none is felt. The footsteps (generated by an intricate set of speakers hidden behind vents near the floor) fade away as rapidly as they came.

'So not just yet,' thinks Alfred, appreciating the buildup.

After returning to his room, Alfred now heads left towards Room Twelve, which he will find bright and unlocked, much to his relief. The brightness does not radiate from the lamps, however, but from an old projector replaying a short video clip of a black-and-white, 1920s style silent cartoon.

The cartoon's title: *The Adventures of Bell Boy!*

A rather jolly and animated young man jumps out of a door labelled '14'. He sprints down the dark corridor with an exaggerated grin on his face, his gaze frantically searching for something on the floor. He finally finds his prize—his tongue, flapping around on its own like fish out of water. The Bell Boy reattaches the tongue into this throat, and with a satisfied grin he clicks his fingers—turning the lamps of the corridor bright in an instant.

As the clip replays, Alfred puts together the narrative.

'So that was the Bell Boy,' he concludes, remembering the footsteps.

The Bell Boy holds the key to brightening up the D.B.I, and whatever is required for this to happen is located within Room Fourteen, two doors across to the left.

Room Thirteen, though unlocked, is pitch black. There seems to be a secondary barricade barring him from entry, though he can hear a soft yet raspy breathing coming from within. This, of course, is the Long Staying Patron, and lucky for Alfred their encounter will not begin just yet.

Alfred arrives at his destination and—to his surprise—finds the Bell Boy in the flesh.

The craftsmanship on display here, at least in my opinion, is on the same level as that of the murdered boy in Room Fifteen. According to sources, the human body takes an unsightly form when left hung by the neck for too long. Post rigor mortis, the sphincter and the associated muscle groups relax, causing the body to soil itself. The tongue, which is a curiously long organ, droops down from the mouth for at least a foot or two, depending on the angle of the rope. The face is puffy with a navy hue, a bare display of the agony felt during the deceased's final moments.

And so hangs the Bell Boy before Alfred, the dribble of his excrement forming a tiny pool on the floor beneath him.

'I think I know what I have to do.'

The thought does cross his mind. Having interpreted the not-so-complicated message behind the cartoon, Alfred has put two and two together. He is averse to the idea, however, namely for two reasons:

(a) He does not really wish to *touch* that; and

(b) The note in his room told him to refrain from touching anyone (although, it did say "refrain from", rather than "do not").

It is for polite guests such as Alfred that we decided to leave a note on the stool, as a little form of encouragement.

Cat got your tongue?

It reads. And around this sentence, the page is filled black with:

Pull it, pull it, pull it, pull it, pull it, pull it.

And so Alfred obliges, and to his disgust the tongue rips out from the back of the Bell Boy's throat, revealing a length which is double that of what he expected. (Alfred is not a squeamish man, but having tested the mechanism personally, I can attest that the sensation is quite something else.)

With the fleshy prize in hand, Alfred now returns to the darkened corridors, awaiting the reemergence of the frantic footsteps. This is a waiting game, and we make Alfred wait for a little longer than he is comfortable with.

The Bell Boy arrives eventually, but this time, halts right in front of him.

Silence.

Alfred holds out the severed tongue in a rather awkward motion.

Some more silence.

Alfred wonders whether he has misinterpreted the puzzle and, being aware of the ever present eyes-in-the-sky, whether the staff overlooking him are chuckling at his daftness.

Seconds pass with no apparent sign of progress.

'Am I doing the right—?'

Click.

And just like that, light is restored to the D.B.I.

Sunken cost theory, as explained by Mr. K, is a tendency among gamblers to 'invest' further into a losing table, upon the mistaken belief that enough investment is due to yield a justified return. Having been a troubled gambler myself I knew all about this, and the purpose behind the Bell Boy could be addressed in similar terms. The lack of vision in these very early stages acts as a roadblock to fully enjoying the D.B.I—a roadblock which the guest themselves must overcome. Having 'invested' some effort and brainpower in solving the puzzle that is the Bell Boy, the guest now seeks reward—in the form of entertainment of course—much more actively as opposed to passively.

The only difference is that the D.B.I is not a fallacy—the more attention one pays to the attractions, the more one will get out of them. And such is the nature of the subsequent part of Alfred's journey, as he is let free to roam the hallways, exploring the premises at his own choosing. The first thing to catch his eye is a gargantuan portrait of an old man, located on the wall along the corridor. As tall as Alfred himself, the portrait is guarded by protective glass and seems to be installed into the physical infrastructure itself, which is unlike any of the numerous paintings that exist in the Inn.

Alfred ponders whether he has seen the old man before, and thinks of the shaman in the storybook: The Fox Sister.

Another feature that catches his eye is the red-painted gates to the Theatre, located in a foyer area. Locked for the time being, there is a panel to the left that reads: "Price of Admission: Two Bronze Coins", on top of which is a toy chimpanzee with its palm outstretched, beckoning payment.

'A treasure hunt,' thinks Alfred.

Accordingly Alfred will search every drawers of every room, after which he will check under every bed and inside every closet. He won't find any, however, for if he wants to view the contents of the Theatre, he is going to need to work a little harder than that.

By our estimation, it will take no less than three hours to fully experience the contents of the guest rooms (with the exception of Room One which is not accessible at this stage). Whilst Alfred takes his time in immersing himself with the various mischiefs and tragedies contained within these walls, he has not forgotten the lipstick-stricken napkin that rests in his pocket.

Find me at the Seagull Lounge, tonight.

Suffice to say, the secret admirer behind this

memo will act as a center piece of the main attraction that is the Seagull Lounge. Main attractions, as touched on previously, forms the central route through which the guest must pass in order to make progress, whereas side attractions may be willfully ignored (in this sense, one could say that the run-in with the Bell Boy counts as a main attraction, categorically speaking).

I will now describe these in turn, although where necessary, I must interject with the actual account of events that transpired during our time here. Whilst Alfred is enjoying his time at the D.B.I, the same could no longer be said for the rest of us remaining on the island.

PARTY AT THE SEAGULL LOUNGE

In terms of structural configuration, the Seagull Lounge most definitely stands out as the visual highlight of the evening. Alfred feels a sense of release as he takes in the panoramic view—a stark contrast to the claustrophobic labyrinth he had waded through so far. For one, the ceilings are extremely high with Victorian styled alcoves to match, accentuating the classical grandeur of this rather illustrious party room. Upon the ledges of the alcoves are seagulls—some sitting and some flying by way of nylon suspension, but all of them taxidermized—skin deep reincarnations of the once vibrant sea birds. Their lifeless eyes glint from the radiating shine of the crystal chandelier.

Without the company of fellow guests, whether they be friends or strangers, one may feel rather lonely in this magnificent room—but such is not the case for Alfred. Alfred has plenty of company here.

To his surprise, Alfred finds the room vastly populated—not with people, but with mannequins.

In all their frozen and silent glory, couples swarm the dance floor with hands on hips and arms on shoulders. There is a group of sharply dressed gentlemen at the bar discussing business, whilst the lively looking bartender shakes them up a cocktail. Waiters in uniforms move swiftly in between tables as they serve the hungry patrons, as the band on the corner stage rocks up a tune: a soft yet jovial 1930s jazz piece.

They're all just mannequins obviously, standing still without an ounce of commotion. Even without actual movement, however, the atmosphere captured here seems to invoke a scene from an era past: a snapshot of what would have been a usual night out at the famed Seagull Lounge.

Alfred notices a poster on the wall:

A lady's true intentions are never spoken out loud!

A clue? Perhaps, thinks Alfred, as he turns his attention to the memo on the napkin. One of these guests is unlike the others, and naturally it is Alfred's mission to locate the secret admirer, but not before exploring this splendor of a party room.

The only thing unsettling about his environment is the expression on the guests' faces. If there is such a thing as an 'aggressive smile', then such a smile has been replicated perfectly on the mannequins' visage. Wading through these overtly happy partygoers, Alfred discovers an aluminum door to the back of the stage labelled: *Kitchen*. There is a numbered padlock on the door, and Alfred would be correct in assuming that figuring out the combination is the key to progress. He continues searching for the admirer.

The truth, however, is that Alfred has already found her.

There is a woman sitting alone at a table at the center of the Lounge, and she is *very* unlike any of the other guests. For one, the entirety of her face is hidden behind a wedding veil. Her physical posture, unlike the stiff rigidity of all the other mannequins, seems limp and fluid, as if an actual corpse has been propped upon the chair underneath her. Her presence is so blatantly conspicuous that Alfred cannot help but feel that she is a trap: a flagrant distraction to keep him from discovering other vital clues hidden in the room.

There are no traps here, fortunately. Or unfortunately, as Alfred is about to find out.

He lifts her wedding veil and screams for the first time.

It's a dead woman. An actual body of a dead woman.

(Subjectively speaking, of course. The craftsmanship utilized here is *extremely* intricate.)

After coming to grips with the impossibility of the scenario, he regains his composure and chuckles. He searches for the surveillance camera and meets our eyes.

'You got me there,' he thinks, as he takes a seat across his apparently deceased partner.

She is caked in makeup, which in turn helps to accentuate the wrinkles on her cheeks and forehead, branching out like the bottom of a dried-up riverbed. Her eyes are pale and without focus, like that of a mackerel past its date of freshness, and the lipstick on her mouth (with which she has created the memo, no doubt) has been applied crudely, as if a toddler was let free with a crimson crayon. Her left hand, just as veiny and lifeless as her face, lies outstretched on the table palms down—as if she is awaiting an engagement ring.

Alfred appreciates the beauty across the table, and while he examines the details, seconds turn to minutes. The inevitable question follows:

'What now?'

The level of difficulty of the puzzle that is about to follow had been greatly debated amongst the founders of the D.B.I. When laid out in writing (as I am about to do), the clues provided and the consequent solutions seem straightforward—no rocket science by any means. However, one had to be cautious when trying to gauge 'perceived' difficulty as opposed to 'actual' difficulty; the guest may not be so receptive to the hints at hand, and it was not our intention to turn this into a test of intellect.

Silent contemplation, at times, reveals more than active pursuit, and Alfred is now beginning to realize that there is something 'off' about the background music.

There is a skip—which Alfred had previously considered a glitch—but the skips are happening routinely, all invariably leading to the rather catchy yet repetitive chorus.

He listens to the lyrics.

Then he grins, as he looks across the table at his secret admirer.

"Take my hand, baby. Kiss it so gently."

He casts a glance at the surveillance camera and raises his eyebrows, as if to silently announce to us: 'Well, here it is.'

He takes the lady's outstretched hand. It feels as cold as it looks. The powdery scent of her make-up strikes his nostrils, and the smell reminds Alfred of his long-deceased grandmother, which he finds abjectly uncomfortable.

He leans forward and, as instructed, gently plants a kiss on the back of the hand.

Click.

The lights go out.

Click.

The lights come back on.

Everyone is staring at Alfred.

The dancers on the floor, the gentlemen at the bar, the waiters, the bartender: everyone.

Everyone except the dead lady in front of him.

"BRING ME!"

She *lunges* at Alfred with a thunderous shriek.

I should point out that Alfred's chair is fixed to the floorboard. This serves two purposes:

(a) To ensure Alfred's correct positioning once we had turned all the heads of the mannequins (accomplished through electric wires via sockets on their soles); and

(b) To ensure Alfred doesn't fall from his chair and break his neck.

The woman, having shocked the daylights out of her bewildered partner, slinks back into her chair, her milky eyes staring blankly at the ceiling as she chants a combination beneath her raspy breath.

"Zero… Two… Three… Five… Six… Nine."

Alfred, being the anecdotal hero of this narrative, makes the immediate connection between her words and the padlock to the Kitchen.

Curiously, however, it is here where many others, who had up until this point ploughed through the various tasks and challenges with flying colors, decide to either retire to their home room of Room Eleven, or make attempts to quit the D.B.I altogether. The simple answer (as garnered by Matt directly) was that the guests had experienced quite enough: ever since boarding the yacht it had been a long and eventful day on the island and, being physically tired (and mentally exhausted in some instances), they were satisfied with the entertainment provided thus far and saw no loss in forfeiting.

Having sat on the chair as an experimental guinea pig, I personally believe that it is the gawking stare of those aggressively smiling mannequins that throw guests off, much more so than the screaming lady. Notwithstanding the blatant grotesquerie that decorate the premises, the mere experience of being stared at by fifty pairs of soulless eyes induced a refreshing type of terror—a sensation that is hard to come by in a more conventional of horror attractions.

Alfred reaches for the padlock, but quickly realizes that the puzzle has yet to be solved.

"Zero… Two… Three… Five… Six… Nine."

The padlock has a four-number combination. The lady is stating six. The aforementioned difficulty of this exercise is at play here, but for those who are keen and attentive enough, the solution can be discovered nearby. Alfred glances at the poster again:

A lady's true intentions are never spoken out loud!

"Zero… Two… Three… Five… Six… Nine."

A brief contemplation discloses the following:

Zero, (One), Two, Three, (Four), Five, Six, (Seven), (Eight), Nine.

And with this four-number combination the padlock opens with a *clink,* revealing white floor tiles made of enamel and stainless-steel walls. Before Alfred makes his entry into the Kitchen, however, the still croaking admirer has one more reminder to add.

"Bring me back my baby gold…"

TREASURE IN THE KITCHEN

As previously exemplified by JY's contribution towards the Long Staying Patron, it was not uncommon for inspiration from staff members to seep into the Inn's attractions. As for the Kitchen, the inspiration therein was not offered but withdrawn, the obvious subject being our star chef Big Cuz. Big Cuz was an easy going man—outside his domain, that is. True to his form, he governed his kitchen with a foul mouth and even fouler temper; the occasional tirades between him and Mr. K. were quite the spectacle to behold. He once jokingly told me about his self-regulated mandate called the "fifty fuck quota": the profanity had to be uttered a minimum of fifty times a day in order to keep his gentle soul at peace.

This aspect of Big Cuz's personality (albeit with a little exaggeration) is well reflected in the notebook that Alfred finds upon entering the Kitchen.

'Clammy and humid' is the theme of this realm, and the contrast of atmosphere with the previous areas of the Inn is immediate. The climate serves well to keep our invertebrate residents alive and thriving—whose identity will be revealed to Alfred soon enough, probably to his dismay.

The notebook seems to belong to a chef with a rather grumpy temperament. In between the order lists for ingredients and manuals for various duties, some personal annotations reveal that the chef is discontent—discontent with his pay, discontent with his staff, discontent with the guests and quite frankly, discontent with everything. The imbeciles at head management have ruined his order again (he asked for Caspian sturgeon, not Siberian. Two different places. Who keeps promoting these geographically challenged morons?) No one wants to take blame for it, least of all the hall staff—or the 'Concierge', as they like to call themselves. Their posh uniforms and purple bow ties make them forget the fact that they hold doors and suckle anus for a living—all the whilst it is the chef who commits to the hard graft in this fuming hell hole of a kitchen. And what is the deal with the new Bell Boy? Why is he always smiling? How does he never shut up, and fail to make sense whenever he opens his mouth? Since when was it workplace policy to hire borderline, mentally ill inbreeds and put them in charge of maintaining the corridor lights? By god, the chef could pay a fortune to punch that stupid grin off his mug.

The Bell Boy should go kill himself. The chef would gladly watch—or help, if so inclined.

Let's not forget the guests, however. Two months

has passed since that boy in Room Fifteen had been abandoned at the hotel—why hasn't he been kicked out? If the owners can afford another freeloader, why can't they afford a much deserved pay raise? Speaking of freeloaders, what on earth is that *thing* that they keep alive in Room Thirteen? Have people seen its face? And why do they keep feeding it caviar? Do they realize how expensive this is? Has everyone lost their minds?

Alfred's gaze scans past these endless tirades, as he hears a faint yet distinct *buzz* that emanates from the deep end of the Kitchen.

The chef's most recent malady, which is to be taken in all seriousness, is that someone has been messing with his money. Some sneaky fingered crook has been stealing from his purse: yesterday he had five coins, and today he has four. His coworkers (who, as a matter of reasonable doubt, could well be in on the crime) keep telling him that he is paranoid. They keep telling him that he slipped it somewhere and simply forgot to retrieve it—the imaginary thief being but a figment of his irritable mental state. But the chef knows better than to trust any of these double-dealing miscreants. And the more he tries to figure out the potential perpetrator, the more his mind gravitates towards the Bell Boy and his stupid grin. It is a veil, the chef convinces himself. A façade of innocence, used to beguile the naive and unknowing. Hidden behind his moronic appearance is a cunning modus operandi: by snatching one or two coins at a time he does not raise alarm, thereby avoiding suspicion as he continues to indulge in his misdeeds. The thought of the Bell Boy rummaging through his belongings makes his blood boil and his insides crawl.

He could strangle the little fuck. Strangle him, hang his corpse from the ceiling beams to cover his tracks, and then he would rip out his tongue and—

The notes become scrambled for here onwards, turning quite indecipherable. They eventually end in a simple yet emphatic fashion:

Must. Hide. The money. They'll never find it.

Alfred closes the notebook.

The buzzing from the other end of the Kitchen is now beginning to get insistent. Turning a corner, Alfred discovers a vast array of glass cabinets with plastic frames, mounted on top of some machinery powered by a whirling fans. These are refrigerators, no doubt, and they contain various ingredients ranging from meat, fish and fungus—all patiently awaiting their turn to be transformed into decadent meals. Their current state, however, can aptly be described as inedible.

In the first cabinet, a sturgeon hangs by its tail. The poor shark however seems to have suffered from acute nuclear radiation—it possesses two heads for a start, and the hue of its belly shines neon pink, with a cavernous gash sliced through its midsection. Thousands of tiny black pearls froth from within, a gleaming sac of mucus barely holding them in place. An amusing display, one may think—a twisted yet imaginative work of silicone craftsmanship. What catches Alfred off guard are the flies.

The flies are real. Alfred had seen them all his life—almost every day in fact, as would have anyone who lives outside the Arctic circle. He is more than familiar with their sporadic maneuvers—the rapid speed with which they crawl across surfaces while rubbing their front feet in devious glee. By all honest accounts these flies are real, and they swarm the caviar in a chaotic throng. Some even seem to be mating.

This is the result of the aforementioned toil called 'fly-catching.' A simple marinade of cooking oil and brown sugar keeps these pests interested on the surfaces of our choosing—being the caviar in this instance. The caviar itself is made of silicone, of course, but the addition of living critters and their ensuing commotion breathes vitality into what would otherwise be considered an inanimate rubber model.

At least, that is the intended effect.

The next cabinet in line contains a woman's head. Various forms of mushrooms grow on it; Alfred can make out Porcini, Oyster, morels and Matsutake (which he recalls having for lunch that afternoon). This cage too is swamped with flies, and unlike its seafaring neighbor, the presence of a human body part enhances the insects' repulsive appeal. A dozen flies come pouring out of the woman's left eye socket and scurry back into her nostrils, eliciting an involuntary itch along Alfred's esophagus.

And as he continues down the aisle Alfred picks up on the off-putting familiarity. Caviar from a twin headed sturgeon. Mushrooms grown from a human head. Rotten scallops. A salmon with three eyes. Various limbs and body parts that may yield unidentifiable morsels of meat.

Alfred has eaten these. They were all part of his menu during lunch and dinner earlier in the day, and having quite enjoyed those meals, Alfred regrets making such a connection. These unappetizing displays provide sufficient enough distraction, but Alfred must now turn his mind to the mission at hand.

One of these cabinets are not like the others. In rumination of Alfred's journey through the D.B.I so far, solutions to puzzles such as these should come intuitively, albeit with a modest twist. This means that the chef's hidden stash must be concealed within one of these cabinets—the challenge being the physical act of retrieving it.

One of these cabinets, unlike the others, is unlocked. And unlike the others, the human torso contained within is not brimming with flies, but what seem to be—to Alfred's immediate perception—maggots.

In truth these are beetle worms, commonly

known as "mealworms" to the few of us that keep reptilian companions as household pets. Sold in various specialized pet stores across the country, mealworms were affordable and in steady supply, and unlike their winged neighbors who co-occupy the Kitchen, these squirmy chums were perfectly hygienic, almost to the point of human consumption. Rumor has it that our predecessors at the Inn attempted to create the display with actual maggots, but were unsuccessful (much to our luck): maggots are curiously fragile creatures and when treated with love and attentiveness, there was little to prevent them from hatching into their rather robust adult forms. To Alfred's eyes however, the worms' nature of origin seems to make little difference as they writhe away in disjointed harmony, welcoming his touch like a warm plate of respiring noodles.

I will spare the details of how Alfred retrieves the coins from this heaping mess. For the average guest this takes more than a couple of tries, after which they will invariably return to their bathroom in Room Eleven to give their hands (and their newly found treasure) a furious wash.

In my personal observation, this marks the point of no return. No guest has willingly forfeited their stay at the Inn past this ordeal, regardless of whether they had enjoyed their time so far. Sunken cost theory has taken its hold, and the lone wanderer will continue on, dragging one tired step after another, till the remaining secrets of the Inn are all but disclosed.

"We've got a problem."

Mr. K and I were in the middle of ironing tablecloths when Big Cuz stormed in. The sun had barely risen, and with it should have arrived a shipment of Yellow Finn Tuna at our shores, ready to be served for the afternoon's patron. What came instead—in the words of Big Cuz—was a box containing substandard, out of season, milky-eyed bullshit without an ounce of fat to be found on its belly.

"The tuna main—it's fucked. I have to go with the risotto."

"You're the chef," replied Mr. K., clearly not in full grasp of the issue at hand.

When it came to risotto our star chef had a mandate: "once the stock hits the pot, you never ever stop"—meaning that a chef was never to leave its side once the rice began cooking. The risotto deserved one's unbridled and undivided attention, and being the calculating kitchen tyrant that he was, Big Cuz always planned his course accordingly when the dish was on the menu, so as to not disrupt his precise modus operandi.

This morning was obviously not the case.

"I need a hand," said Big Cuz, casting a glance at my direction, and was immediately challenged with Mr. K.'s protests.

I was on full roster for the night, and as employee wages were firmly set to this roster, Mr. K. was not about to let his junior get overworked without proper consultation or compensation—let alone in a field where he had no expertise in.

"I'll do it."

They both looked at me in surprise. Never before had I cut off Mr. K. in the middle of a sentence.

"I'll do it," I repeated, as I hastily (though neatly) pushed aside my tablecloth.

"We're not about to let a guest lunch go to shit, right?"

And thus began what I like to consider the second phase of my time on the island, and also—though in retrospect, what I consider the first step in to my current career. I must admit, cooking for a single guest in no way reflects the anxiety-ridden pressure of working in a fine dining kitchen, but the level of precision and commitment required was well instilled within me. It began with the ingredients—what was in season, out of season, how sweet a rhubarb should taste during early Spring and how firm a sea bass should feel hours after rigor mortis. I had already acquired the rudimentary basics of working in a kitchen by this point (such as dates, labels, orders, hygiene), but under Big Cuz's official tutelage this hit a whole new level. No longer was I expected to simply follow instructions (which can be arduous enough), but I was required to have 'vision'—a thorough understanding of the menu, the service, and all the menial grind work necessary to achieve a successful dinner. Big Cuz didn't stop there—he took the same ethos to the preparation of staff meals, so that I may experience some volume under pressure. Everyone was shocked at the sudden jump in quality of the 'family meal', despite the price of the ingredients remaining as modest as before. This, of course, came at the expense of hard work, but I wasn't about to let that get in the way of what I considered to be an invaluable experience.

Slowly but naturally, my name tag was shifting from Concierge to Sous Chef.

The only downside of this was that I became further separated from Matt, who was still dutifully fulfilling his role as the Inn's nighttime operator. No doubt I considered him my closest friend on the island (and a close friend in general), but with myself now working daylight hours, time for interaction was stifled, and so was our mutual topics of discussion. It was for this reason, I believe, that his gradual withdrawal into recession went unnoticed—or to be precise, untended. He still shielded himself behind his dry humor and laid-back attitude, but the very notion that he was 'shielding' anything bothered me, and for the longest time there was nothing I could do.

So one Thursday, at the break of dawn, I joined him for a run.

"You sure, mate?" he asked. "Not to be rude but you've kind of grown a belly. I'm not slowing down for you, and I don't want you to have a heart attack."

And so the run became a race, and no surprise to anyone, Matt blitzed me into oblivion.

Panting like the unfit slob I was, I crossed the finish line as Matt waited for me, arms folded. I believe it was the first time in a month where I actually saw him smile. Outside the perfunctory jabs and insults, we didn't discuss anything in particular on our way back to the Resort. We didn't need to— at least in my mind. Matt knew how much I despised these early morning exercises, and the very fact that I turned up was a statement in and of itself. All things considered, I think he appreciated it.

It was the dead pan glare of Mr. K. that greeted us when we returned.

"I have… something important to discuss with you."

We looked at each other in confusion.

"*Both* of you. I'll see you in my office in five."

This was odd. Despite knowing that Matt and I were personal friends, Mr. K. always kept it professional when discussing 'important matters'— such as employment, benefits, work performance and the like. He expected us to keep these confidential with equal professionalism, so it was extremely uncharacteristic of him to call us into his office in tandem.

Oh, we told each other through our eyes when we reached the same conclusion.

We're about to get fired.

We had touched on this topic before. As far as we were aware, D.B.I had been in operation for just over a decade. Ten years is a fair run for any standalone business, no matter how large a capital that had been invested into its development. And when I say 'business' I say it with partial sincerity, for by this time we had realized that the Inn was more of a passion project for the wealthy proprietor (or a 'vanity project', whichever description one prefers), and less of a well oiled profit-making machine. With a target market as specific as the D.B.I—that being (rich) horror enthusiasts—it was only natural that the lifespan of this grand contraption was closing to an end.

Don Jiral had run its course, and as a result, heads were about to roll.

"JY was involved in a traffic accident," said Mr. K.

We stood there in silence for a moment.

"And she is okay?" asked Matt.

"She had been in a coma."

This insufficient statement should have been followed by a barrage of questions, but it wasn't. Mr. K. had neither answered Matt's question, nor had he given an adequate explanation as to why this information was being conveyed to us now, and in this manner. The expression on his face barred us from speaking, but eventually one of us broke the silence, though I cannot remember who.

"And?"

Two days of bereavement leave was granted to Matt to attend the funeral, which he refused. Though I never asked, I think I understood why. For Matt, the mainland meant 'reality' (in quotation marks, for what this exactly meant to him one could only guess), and nothing could force him more to face this concept as to attend JY's last rites. As we stood on the hill to the side of the Resort, I could offer no consolation. The crimson sunset stretched in the horizon and all I could do was stare at it, not uttering a word. It crossed my mind to convince Matt to attend the service, but the notion that it was not my place to do so, coupled with my own shock at what had just occurred, froze me to inaction. Looking back, perhaps this was my last chance to alter the ensuing events on the island—if such thing was a possibility in the first place. We spent the rest of the evening on the hill, watching the grey waves as the they rolled into the harbor.

The body washed up on shore on Sunday morning.

And to everyone's absolute fright and astonishment, it was that of Mr. K.

The police tried their utmost to keep things under a wrap, but on an island (and community) as small as this, details tend to leak rather effortlessly.

'Open and shut case,' is how one staff described it, as the body was wearing swimming shorts and goggles, with no signs of external trauma or wounds. The deceased had gone for a swim only to be caught in a rip tide—and in the ensuing darkness he likely lost his bearing, as he struggled against the water until his limbs (then his lungs) gave out.

"Open and shut case—my ass," was everyone else's reaction.

Mr. K. never went for swims. Not only that, the configuration of the shores on this island made it difficult for anyone to even imagine the idea of going for a swim. With no adequate beaches to speak of, the notion of Mr. K. standing on a pier, in his swimming shorts and goggles (which we had no idea he even possessed), diving into the murky waters never to return, painted such a bizarre picture in everyone's minds that it was only natural for us to reject such a scenario.

It was only then I realized how little any of us really knew about Mr. K—outside his role as the Head Concierge. I assume upper management dealt with whatever that needed to be 'dealt with', but it was done with such efficiency that the event caused no commotion to the smooth-running of the business at all. Of course, proper respect and condolences were given where it was due. A man in a suit (whom none of us had met before) came over from headquarters to present a few words following a moment of silence in his memory, but oddly enough no information was given as to the details of his funeral service. Perhaps this was due to a difference in work culture, but having never lost a workmate to an accident since, I still cannot say for sure whether this was customary.

Rumors, as they often do, spread like algae on a pond—or in this instance, more like an Australian bushfire in the middle of May.

The wife divorced him and took all his assets, said one such rumor.

Nonsense, responded another. Then why the need for all this swimming fiasco?

Life insurance is where it's at—it must be. He needed to stage this as an accident to be eligible for cover.

Was he desperate for money? Why? Failed business deal? Creditors? Loan sharks after him, threatening his family? It makes sense why there is no funeral service then, doesn't it?

"Fuck it all," said Big Cuz. "Fuck it. It's not our fucking place to second guess anything about him. We remember him just as he was. That's what he would have wanted."

Despite the profanity, I found this approach to be the most sensible and mature—not to mention humane. Coming from a man who was often at odds with Mr. K., the stoic respect Big Cuz showed here hit differently altogether. As such, I never discussed the issue with anyone on the island, even Matt. The subject of Mr. K.'s now vacant role, however, became relevant after a short period of time.

Matt had volunteered to be the new Head Concierge.

Clink, clink.

Upon Alfred placing the two bronze coins into the palm of the chimpanzee, the control center unlocks the gate to the Theatre. Beyond the red doors there are about a dozen leather seats, all facing a modestly large screen that flickers every so often. What will play for him now is a documentary (or more accurately, a pseudo-documentary—in consideration of its fictional nature) that briefly describes the history of the island. The footage and photographs used are, in honesty, a hodge-podge of antique, low resolution material which have been heavily edited to suit our story. What sells it, in my belief, is the narrator—whom I hear was quite a big name in the Korean educational and history channels. They say a lot of convincing took place to employ this man, for the specific accounts he is about to recite are not altogether fictitious— evidenced by sporadic historical records that are alarmingly close to contemporary times.

A BRIEF HISTORY ON THE ISLAND OF IKKA-DO

[Blight, by its inevitable nature, finds its place in the history of all cultures and all peoples. For those who claim heritage in the Korean peninsula, such a concept may be related to war, strife, foreign annexation—and more recently, political scandal and systematic corruption. None, however, would go so far (or even fathom in remote seriousness) as to associate the blight on this land with the ritualistic act of human sacrifice.

The first records of inhabitation on the Island of Ikka-do appear in 1621, although many assume that civilization existed there much earlier. There are a few hypotheses as to why people settled on such a minute and unyielding land, one of them being that the population descended from a community of exiles. The stigma would explain why they never left —despite the soil being too salty to offer crops and the waters too rough to safely fish from. The most destructive of all were the seasonal storms, which thoroughly and routinely flattened what humble semblance of infrastructure the poor settlers managed to raise.

Perhaps it was the island's unforgiving temperament that turned its inhabitants equally merciless. As the adage goes, desperate times call upon drastic measures, and in the case of Ikka-do, the measures utilized need not adhere to scientific rationale nor basic morality.

The method is documented with disturbing precision. The preferred subject is an infant under one hundred days old, but in their absence, toddlers were used. The body is covered from head to toe in sulfur, as to imitate the radiance of gold—but the mouth and nose should be kept clear, for the gift only has effect when offered still breathing. The subject is then sealed within a large ceramic pot, the kind normally used to ferment and store pickles— with tiny breathing holes. A designated watcher, which was often the subject's mother, would come around every hour and speak to the subject, tapping on the pot and checking for life. Should the subject be old enough to understand language, the mother must promise swift rescue, encouraging the child to bear the pain a little while longer. Arguably the most deplorable detail of all is the following description:

"This is to simultaneously heighten the conflicting notions of hope and dread, for the more mental anguish the gift endures, the tastier of an offering the gift becomes."

At dawn, the entirety of the island would gather on the shore and bow down before a portrait of a shaman. At daybreak the pot is cast into the waters

—at which point, if the pot sinks (which it always did), a year of good climate and fruitful harvest would be granted upon the island. Each time the ritual took place, a stone statue of the baby (in the figure of an angel) was raised in its recognition.

It is hotly debated as to the precise time of when this practice began and when it ended, although sources agree that the approximate period coincides with the arrival of a foreigner—referred to as, among many other things, a shaman, a priest, or "Goo Seh Joo", translating to Messiah, just as in the Christian Bible. By all accounts, notwithstanding one's belief in divine intervention or environmental climate change, the remedy seemed to have worked: the storms simply *ceased* from the early 1700s. Cross-checking by eager historians and doubtful skeptics alike were entirely possible, since hurricanes of such magnitude were routinely felt upon the mainland coast, and accounts were kept accordingly. But for the gentle rain in the spring and the forgiving winter snow, the island, in the sense of primal existence, became a paradise.

Untested remedies are not without their side effects however, and the ritual that safeguarded Ikka-do seemed no exception. Its inhabitants, for lack of a better term, turned insane. The symptoms came subtly and appeared to affect a designated few. It came in disguise, such as drowning incidents when young men went swimming in the middle of a winter night. No foul play, supernatural or otherwise, was suspected at first: the audacity of youngsters have propensity to cause dangerous outcomes—even fatal ones in the worst of scenarios. When the exact same incident began happening to the elderly, people began questioning.

Homicide occurred for the most minuscule of reasons in the most extreme of fashions. Neighbors decapitated each other over stolen beans, and mothers strangled their toddlers for wetting their beds. For a community as enclosed as the one on the isle, a functioning justice system may have been too much to ask, but even in the most outlying of human settlements, 'frontier justice' usually played a role. No such thing existed on Ikka-do. According to the surviving sources, punishment for crimes—even the most violent of crimes—were seldom exacted. But when they were, the subject under trial were fried alive in sesame oil, always at the foot of the portrait of the shaman, with the whole village in attendance in ceremonious fashion.

1953 marked the end of the Korean war, though nation wide recovery would take place years later, and modernization much down the line. It wasn't until the 1970s when the country embarked on a thorough census of the islands on the relatively less developed parts of the coast, by which time the median age of Ikka-do was seventy-five.

"There just aren't no more," said one woman, according to the 1975 national census. "The gifts— there just aren't no more. The ones we've been offering are stale. Please."

The area was depopulated in 1993, and commercialization began in the 2001.]

The reel ends with a looping footage—villagers kneeling before a gigantic painting of a shaman, rubbing their palms together in prayer. It is exact same painting that lies fixed into the wall, just a minute's walk away from Alfred's current location.

IN THE BELLY OF THE BEAST

The name is truly cliché, but as an internal reference we found no better alternative. Notwithstanding the varying degree of pride each of us had for our workplace, we all agreed that the D.B.I—as haunted attractions go—offered something unique: something to evoke one's imagination as well as challenge their mental agility. It was also agreed, however, that the journey up to this point—consisting of whimsical puzzles, broken narratives, and the occasional sprinkle of gore and insects—severely lacked an emphatic sense of *oomph*. No matter how unique the business, a "haunted house" had a slogan to live up to, and lest the guest depart partly satisfied, certain thirsts had to be quenched.

This is where you get the *oomph*.

This is where you fulfill all yearning for jump scares and cheap thrills—without a doubt, it is a place of unilateral sensory bombardment.

Alfred, well trained in the arts of the Inn by now, kneels and prays before the portrait—ensuring that the all-seeing eye has clear vision of his humble disposition. At the press of a button the visage swings open, as the giant frame unlatches itself to form a doorway into the basement. Alfred peers into the gloom.

From the pit of the belly echoes a concoction of howls. One sound is distinct on the outermost layer —a groaning of a man—and as Alfred descends further it becomes evident that the groan is not one of pain, but of ecstasy.

There is a bull, laying to the right side of the staircase atop a mound of hay, innards ripped open.

"Oh," says the animatronic, rolling its eyes and quivering its lips. *"I deserve to die like this. Oh, God."*

The jump scare, naturally, comes in from the left. A fair amount of contemplation went into the design of the Fox Sister, whose origin—the nine tailed fox prevalent in East Asian folklore—tended to materialize in the form of a sultry beauty, at least in contemporary pop-culture. We wanted none of that.

So the chosen design was simply that of a giant fox. Clutched between its teeth however, was a severed head of a girl—and the girl was the one who did the talking.

"Lay down with me?" she asks Albert, eyes bleeding. *"I don't hurt anyone. Lay down with me? I don't hurt anyone. Lay down with me? I don't -"*

The fox *crunches* its jaws shut, grinding the girl's head into a pulp. It slinks away into the shadows, its cheerful giggle lingering in the air for the duration of the descent.

"It's naïve," thunders a voice, just as Alfred reaches the pit of the belly. "People sign a registration form and swipe their little credit cards, then think it's all safe and dandy. Do you know where you *are?*"

Curtains of hair droop from the ceiling, obscuring vision.

"That's real hair, by the way, brushing against your cheeks right now. Barbers used to practice with them, but allegedly they're bad luck. Do you know where you *are?*"

Alfred navigates under the flashing strobe lights.

"Page three, paragraph two. The Guest—that'd be you, Alfred—acknowledges any and all risks arising from the usual operation of the Premises, including but not limited to, accidental death and injury for any and all reasons not in connection with preventable mechanical faults owing to gross negligence of the Host—that'd be us—and the Guest waives for the Host any and all liability in relation to said death and injury, and indemnifies and holds harmless the Host for any and all claims, actions or injunctions brought on by a Third Party. Whew, that's a mouthful. As to why anyone would sign this thing, I have no idea. Do you know where you *are?*"

Seagulls shriek from the ceiling beams—picking at the eye sockets of senior citizens. Their heads dangle like cured meats on a hook. *My boy,* one of them mutters.

"I hope you like the taste of the ocean in April—the waves are extra frothy around this time of the year. We don't know much about you, Alfred, but we've been keeping a very close eye on you these past few hours. Oh, how we would love to pick your brains for a little while longer. But we have a task for you—and we are very pleased indeed that you seem capable of the job. Do you know where you *are?*"

The wailing stops.

The spotlights fixate at the center of the basement. There is an altar, upon which lies a replica of a woman with the head of a goat, nine months into pregnancy.

"And do you know what you have to *do?*"

In short, Alfred must now perform a cesarian section with his bare hands. There is a picture manual to help him understand, but I'll spare the details.

Clink.

The lights go off.

"Do you think this is a joke? Do you think this is entertainment? *Is this entertaining for you?* We're going to die, we're going to die, if we don't keep up traditions we're all going to die. Traditions are important, didn't your parents teach you why traditions are important? You are never leaving this basement. You are never leaving this island. Oh stale, so stale, the offerings so stale—"

The audio cuts off, and brightness returns.

Jesus, I had expressed my concerns at first. *Isn't this borderline abuse?*

Out of context, perhaps. This is the point in the journey where trust becomes important: trust that the host will keep the environment 'safe'—and trust that the guest won't be overtly offended. At the time of writing these accounts, the antics in store at the Basement would likely be considered unduly distasteful (even by the standards of a 'haunted house'), but as with any censorship applicable to facets of entertainment, I can only to repeat the tired adage: times seem to have changed. After all, the guests *did* sign themselves up for a night in a "Drowned Baby Inn"—and if I may be so brazen, it would be rather disingenuous of them to reject infantile horror.

Alfred rips the newborn mannequin from the silicone womb. Clutched in the baby's hand is the key to Room One—signaling the final stretch of the long night's adventure, the completion of which would qualify our anecdotal guest into the 'Finishers' Hall of Fame.

I would like to imagine these events in the happiest way possible. As such, JY would still be there, Matt would still be there, and also Mr. K.— and we would wait in the golden lit lobby in eager anticipation of Alfred's triumphant return: champagne glasses ready for our esteemed guest and Finisher.

Room One is in fact no room, but an exit: a

tapered hallway leading to a spiral of rusty stairs, the descent of which leads Alfred to an oddly foreign environment: outside. On the walls of the hallway are murals, painted in sequence as to instruct Alfred on the requirements of the night's finale. A rose petalled labyrinth, sparsely populated with baby angels bearing a smile—and a golden pond located therein.

The murals make it clear that it is Alfred's job to drown the infant here. It won't be the leisurely stroll as he had taken in the afternoon, however: courtesy to our audio system, the entire labyrinth will be blaring with juvenile shrieks, peppered sporadically with a discernible "please, don't". Sometime during the evening, we have also laced the pond with glitters. If his memory and perception serves, Alfred will remember his admirer's prior request: *bring me back my baby gold.*

There is a flashlight placed near the end of the staircase. The Eye in the Sky no longer guarantees his safety, and despite the lengthy disclaimers our guest has had to sign, we surely do not want Alfred falling off a cliff. Torch in one hand, and baby in the other, Alfred sets off into the night.

"Think he'll get it?" asks JY.

"The pond?" Matt responds. "Absolutely. He seems pretty sharp, the way he's handled the puzzles so far—"

"No. I mean the whole *thing*. About why he's here."

This was the question we raised, every time we waited for a Finisher. On more than a few occasions the Finisher would return to the lobby, tired yet triumphant, sit down on the velvet sofa with a champagne glass in hand, and ask:

That was… something else. But what was it all about?

We never disclosed to the guest that the accounts of the *[Brief History of Ikka-do]* were not all fictitious in nature. Sacrifices did happen here—though the details depicted in the pseudo-documentary were exaggerated to add flavor. An ardent researcher may —prior to or after their visit to the D.B.I—find out about the island's sordid past, and allow themselves to ask the question: was it all for entertainment, or is something else at play here?

This was the mystery that was intended to pervade their minds: a lingering curiosity that perhaps, in accordance with their wildest dreams of conspiracy, the business itself was a ruse—an elaborate veil atop a foul tradition, formulated for the purpose of continuing a shamanistic ritual that —in some way or form, whether true or make-belief —served its wealthy owners in ways other than profit.

Come to think of it—in light of everything that occurred after my departure—I couldn't be so sure myself.

We hear the bleep on the radio.

"VIP is returning from the hedge maze. Baby is gold."

"Roger and out," answers Mr. K. "All staff, to your positions. And *please*, for the love of God, co-ordinate the champagne pop this time. Remember: we end on a b-"

"Bang, not a fizzle. Aye, aye, captain," replies Matt, hopping off the barstool. He nudges me and JY with a grin, voice imitating our Head Concierge. "Remember guys, it's three, two, one, then pop. Not three, two, pop. Repeat after me: three, two, one, then pop. Not three, two—"

Bleep.

"VIP is four minutes out."

"Lights down!" yells Mr. K. "Matt, stop being a smart ass and get in position."

And so, in the darkness, we wait.

Three...

Two...

One...

Upon this anecdotal adventure, I choose to consign all my fond thoughts for the D.B.I. Quite a unique attraction indeed—filled with whimsical puzzles and not-so-whimsical display of gore; a paper mâché of peculiar events that stick close enough to hold a narrative, but not so close as to unravel its enigma. A milestone—*two* milestones in fact: one that killed my degenerate (and rather expensive) habit, and another that birthed my current career. As much as we liked to chuckle at the wealthy patrons who graced the establishment—and their Don Jiral ways of spending spare income—in hindsight, I genuinely believe that we wished every guest would enjoy their time here: to truly relish all the quirks and scares in store at the Drowned Baby Inn.

And so, after many hours of trials, tribulations and—of course—entertainment, the night concludes for our esteemed and imaginary friend, Alfred.

Pop.

I had never seen someone get punched so hard in my entire life.

Matt flew across the room. The perpetrator of the assault was none other than Big Cuz.

"Give us a minute," said the chef. In any other situation, I would have retaliated against such an attack upon a friend of mine—especially Matt, who without doubt would have done the same for me. But not this time. Despite my shock at the intensity of the blow, I wholly understood where it originated from—for had Matt been my kin and myself his senior, perhaps I would have delivered the punch myself. I closed the door behind me and gave the two some privacy.

This occurred three weeks into Matt's appointment as Head Concierge. By this time, he had solidified his decision to remain on the island—despite being told of his friend and cousin's imminent departure. To my everlasting gratitude, Big Cuz had recommended me to his former workplace—a well renowned fine dining establishment in Seoul, fortunately in need of a vetted sous chef. Big Cuz had plans to open up a restaurant himself, and should the opportunity allow, we could be working in the same kitchen again in the distant future. As for Matt, we tried to remind him of his own past ambitions. He could teach English, earning a modest living as a private tutor whilst working towards whatever goal he had in sight. Despite his abhorrence towards the idea, the man did hold a law degree so admission to the bar was not off the books. Hell, if things failed to pan out, he could always help as a manager at Big Cuz's restaurant. We tried to remind him of a life outside the island—more careers to be trialed, relationships to be formed and adventures to be had —and towards these notions his answer was a firm, cold and resounding "no thank you."

I should make it absolutely clear here that Big Cuz is no mother-hen when it comes to occupations and career choices. He himself became a chef against the vehement protest of his parents, and outside the tyrannical domain of his kitchen, the man was a free spirit by all accounts. *You should do whatever fucking job you like,* he used to say. *So long as your head is in the right place.* As to this second component, Big Cuz and I were becoming profoundly concerned.

"Where did he go?" asked Matt, entering the dining room.

I looked up, then around. It was me alone in the vacuous hall, folding and ironing tablecloths.

"Where did *who* go?" I asked in return.

Matt examined the room from corner to corner, shrugged, then simply left without providing me with a response. When questioned later he brushed it off with a casual (yet oddly curt) "don't worry about it." From our five years of friendship, I knew Matt to be a 'wisecracker'—comically cynical in his expressions (in an endearing, relatable way) and always finding jokes in the most stressful of situations. But he was never into practical jokes. In the handful of times he tried, it was always so that the recipient appreciated—or at least understood—what was so humorous about the entire ordeal.

Matt genuinely saw someone walk into that dining room, saw him disappear—and was now pretending like it never happened. I wouldn't have worried about this minor incident, if it weren't for the fact that other staff members were noticing how 'strange' Matt was behaving. It did not affect his work ethic or capabilities: on the contrary he was more focused than ever, fulfilling his new role as Head Concierge rather admirably. Outside of his shifts, however, Matt was—to put it mildly—extremely aloof and borderline *weird*: the kind of weird where one might hear him in a room, laughing and chatting, but once intruded upon, he would be found reading a book in complete solitude.

"Can I help you?" he would ask nonchalantly.

"Oh, I thought someone was in here with you," the intruder would respond.

"In here? No? You must have misheard something from down the hall."

Shrugging in confusion, the person would leave —doubtfully questioning their own sense of hearing. And as soon as the door is closed:

"Hahahaha."

Perhaps it was a very funny book. At the time, I did not wish to contemplate any implications based on the contrary. My ears did, however, lend themselves to a freshly formed gossip, scuttering about in the air from the whispers of one staff to another. Despite my aversion towards paying attention to (let alone partaking in) such unsavory discourse, the growing apprehension for my friend swayed me into attaining further details.

It was in relation to Mr. K's predecessor: the first ever Head Concierge at the D.B.I. A well respected man—responsible for setting up our day-to-day work practices that were still in place to date. Four years into service, he drank a pint of weed-killer and died of lung failure.

Police ruled it as an accidental death, as the man was heavily intoxicated at the time of the incident, and had likely consumed the chemical by mistake. (For if suicide was the objective, why take the care to pour it into a glass, and not drink from the bottle itself?) The manner of this haphazard diagnosis seemed quite similar to the one attributed to Mr. K.'s drowning. As tragic as these events were, the staff would not have given further thought, nor spawned deeper rumination about the woeful subject matter—but for the fact that the new man in the role was acting too odd for comfort.

Once is an occurrence. Twice, a coincidence. Three times… well. No-one wanted to know what three times could imply.

For Big Cuz, the straw that broke the camel's back was when Matt began referring to the island as "home." We gathered one night in Matt's room, and though the manner was subtle, Matt made it clear through his intonations that our presence was not altogether welcome.

"You want to stay with this job… Fine. That's your fucking prerogative. But take a holiday at least. Visit your family. Visit home," said Big Cuz.

"Taking a holiday is my 'fucking' prerogative too, isn't it? I don't need one. I feel just at home right here," answered Matt.

"Why the fuck are you acting like this?"

"Acting like what?"

"Acting like everything's all fine-fucking-dandy; acting like *you're* all fine-fucking-dandy, because you're *not*. You've gone through a lot, Matthew. I know I'm not the best guy to console you on shit like this, but let's face it. You've gone through a lot, and you need a break."

"I don't need one."

"I ask this as your big cousin, who's known you since six years old. Do it for me. Take a break. Hop off this island for at least just a week."

"You have no idea what you're talking about, do you?" said Matt.

Silence.

An eerie, uncanny sense of vitriol pervaded the air.

"Listen…" said Big Cuz after a pause. "I'm going to say this at the expense of sounding condescending. You don't understand what's healthy for you right now."

"No, no, *you* don't understand." Matt replied. "I… *belong* here. I belong here. Get this through that thick skull of yours—"

Pop.

Thus the punch was thrown, sending my friend across the room. The message behind the violence was clear: snap out of it. Whatever's going on, please snap the fuck out of it. Seeing Matt rise, both Big Cuz and I realized that the message had failed. His face showed no anger, not even shock. Eyes glazed and expression stoic, he silently repeated his unsettling mandate. *I belong here.*

"Give us a minute," said Big Cuz.

The ensuing few days were by far the worst during my time on the island. Matt, under his authority as

Head Concierge and with the 'just' reason of assault on a colleague, had fired Big Cuz. This was a moot point in terms of operations, as Big Cuz was already scheduled to leave in a week's time. The gesture, however, spoke volumes in antagonism. Matt—the once chummy and laid-back Kiwi lad who was liked by everyone for his cheeky sense of humor—had fired his own family member over a punch; a punch thrown out of care and goodwill, if one were to be completely honest. Baffled at Matt's decision I confronted him, demanding—and in my mind, begging—to know what was truly going on in his head.

"It's according to protocol," was his reply, and refused to grant me further audience.

In the face of this disingenuous response, my own confusion and bewilderment simmered to anger, and we never spoke again on the island. Days crawled by under this unbearable gloom, bringing my time at the D.B.I. to a tiresome close. As I boarded the ferry I gazed back at my "home" of the past many months: the wooden planks of the piers, the granite staircase leading up to the gravel road, stretching far into the rolling meadows peppered with dandelions– and in the distance—the once ominous tree line of birch and pines, concealing the island's main source of attraction—beckoning all visitors towards its horrific delights. *Picturesque,* was the word that came to mind, which sat uncomfortably with the fact that I had lost two colleagues here, and was leaving one behind in irate anxiety.

"So long," I said to myself—or more precisely—to the Inn.

And in this precise moment, something strange occurred. An apprehension—an unfounded yet compelling premonition—that if I were to leave now, all my memories associated with the island—both pleasant and otherwise—would somehow, in some way, fade completely. *Well, that's how memories work,* said the logical part of my brain. *If you don't think about them often enough, they fade.*

But do you want them to?

The revving of the ferry's engine broke me to sobriety. It was a silly sensation to say the least—perfectly natural, some might say, to experience some kind of 'cold-feet' when leaving an endeared workplace, no matter how poorly the tenure had ended. The feeling lasted mere seconds, and never returned. Nevertheless, I must admit the truth of what I felt in that moment: fear—fear of leaving the island, fear of returning to the mainland, fear of no longer being a concierge at the D.B.I. The ferry picked up speed—the ocean gust blasting away what remnants of this irrational fear that lingered at the back of my mind. The island turned into a dot, and soon enough, disappeared completely into the blue horizon.

Needless to say, I remain unaffected (at least to date) by any symptoms of unnatural amnesia. As vivid as they were, I parked these memories far away from conscious thought, for my newfound occupation demanded every ounce of focus I could spare. The only notion that kept creeping to the foreground was that of my departure: the peculiar yet ominous sensation that momentarily bound me to the island, against all good sense and logical judgement. I would ask myself: could I explain it to anyone? Had I been exposed to such phenomena for a prolonged length of time—strengthening each day without understandable cause—could I explain myself to anyone in a coherent manner, let alone justify any decisions I make as a result of such feelings?

Could Matt?

A month into my new job, I invited Big Cuz over for dinner—and took hours to convince him to give Matt a call together. To burrow his expression, he was still "fucked off" about what had happened in the end—though I believe that under his layer of frustration and anger, the man was genuinely hurt over how he had to leave his cousin behind. We reached a compromise: I would call Matt as if I were alone and Big Cuz would listen in. They were kin after all, and despite current enmities he felt an inkling of responsibility to at least check upon Matt's wellbeing.

To my relief, Matt answered my call and better still, he sounded good. 'Good' as in 'normal': the candid, easy-going wisecracker that I knew Matt to be. He asked a great deal about my current job—sympathizing with me over the obscene hours and jokingly predicting that I'd one day sell my soul to the infamous tire company, in exchange for a couple of asterisks on their lofty guidebook.

"Hell, I wish," I said.

"You'll get there. Just don't have an enlightenment and go all vegan on me."

As for the D.B.I, major creative overhauls were taking place. Most of the attractions—even the main ones—were scheduled to receive a complete makeover, and as Head Concierge Matt was helming many of the projects. There was excitement in his voice—genuine enthusiasm for his area of profession—and none of the dreary *I belong here* nonsense he was spewing a month ago. I was truly happy for Matt, for despite still being on the island his head seemed to be in the right place. I looked over, and saw that Big Cuz was in silent agreement.

"Listen," said Matt as our call drew to a close. "I know I should tell him myself and … I know how angry he is at what I did. Could you do me a favor and speak to Big Cuz for me?"

Pause.

"Of course," I answered, my gaze locked with Big Cuz.

"Tell him… Tell him I know he was always looking out for me. Tell him that I'm thankful, and tell him I deserved that punch ten times over. Tell him I'll give him a call to apologize properly. Yeah… please tell him that."

I promised that I would, knowing instantly that any feud or misunderstanding between the two were now over. Big Cuz let out a sigh as I hung up—and though he didn't say outright, I knew he was glad to have relented to my request. Our hearts much lighter than before, we made a final toast and finished our drinks. I had a full-on lunch shift the following day, and Big Cuz was busy scouting locations for his restaurant. Ready to dive back into our daily grind, we concluded the dinner—an evening well spent by all accounts, and we hoped to reconvene again in the near future.

The next time we meet would be at Matt's funeral, three months later.

I must confess at this point, that whilst the primary purpose of recording these events were to relive my experiences on the island, the story undeniably has been—at heart and in sincerity—an ode to my friend now long departed, and the memories we had shared. It was a fulfillment of the hair-raising adventures that we had once so childishly yearned for, and—if one were to look at it through the rosiest of lenses—working at the D.B.I had thoroughly gratified our aspirations. Suffice to say, however, I no longer harbor the desire to visit such establishments. No more horror-attractions, no more haunted houses. Consciously or otherwise, I buried that enthusiasm along with my friend.

Big Cuz picked me up at five in the afternoon. It was an hour's drive to the funeral parlor, but the evening Seoul traffic extended the ride—throughout which we remained silent. The questions that hung over our shoulders were as follows:

Why didn't you do something to stop it?

We did. We tried everything we could.

Everything? Are you sure?

No, we weren't—and that was precisely the cause of our pain. Matt ended his life by hanging himself, along the forest walkway where we used to sweep the leaves. There was no note, but no evidence of foul play either. They say it happened at dawn.

Big Cuz parked the vehicle, but we stayed inside. Seconds passed as both of us struggled to keep those questions from slipping out—those tragic and fearful questions, riddled with sorrow, with regret, and undeniably, guilt. Big Cuz took the courage to speak first.

"I wonder," he said, with great effort. "I wonder what his final thoughts were."

Pause.

He apologized. He said he shouldn't be burdening me like this—he was just thinking out loud and I need not answer. I answered anyway.

"I think..." I began. "I think his final thoughts would have been: I hope I scare the *shit* out of some rich fucker that walks up here this morning."

Pause.

We looked at each other in silence. Then Big Cuz chuckled. Then I chuckled. We laughed: genuinely, we laughed. Not because Matt dying was funny. But because that's precisely the guy we knew him to be. Here was the simple truth: we would never find out what was going on in Matt's mind, and what his reasons were for doing what he did. So we decided not to second guess him. We would choose to remember him just the way he was. I think that's what he would have wanted.

Approaching the funeral house I received a phone call: some urgent matters related to the restaurant, so I excused myself whilst Big Cuz entered first. Concluding the matter as swiftly as I could, I turned to make my entrance—then I saw a man, standing by the door, hair silver and impeccably dressed in a black coat, suit and tie.

It was Matt's father—and the pang of guilt temporarily forgotten came shooting back in inexplicable frenzy. I felt my sense of intelligence degenerate—as if I had somehow forgotten how to greet an elder in proper Korean fashion. Do I bow, and when I bow, what do I say? Hello sir, I'm so sorry for your loss? Do I remind him of who I am, in case he has forgotten? Do I explain that I worked with Matt on the island, and that, given the circumstances, was one of the very few who could've *done something about it?*

To my extreme relief, my bumbling introduction

was met with neither confusion nor frigidity. He remembered who I was, though he was unaware that I had been his son's colleague in recent months. He remembered how close I was to Matt during our university years, and remarked how Matt would talk in great lengths about me, always in very favorable terms. He said he was glad to see me again after all this time, and despite being overwhelmed with grief, the rest of the family would no doubt feel the same. At first, I had feared that this abrupt interaction would further compound my sense of guilt and regret. But the opposite was the case. His eyes glistened with the sorrow of a bereaved father, but there was no anguish behind them—his imposing yet soothing demeanor drawing me deeper into heartfelt condolence.

"Thank you for being a friend to my son," he said.

And at this point, my own composure broke and I wept. Perhaps it was rude of me to do so—I was in the father's presence after all, and my own tactless feeling of grief would have been incomparable to that of a parent. He consoled me all the same, and asked of me a favor—a 'difficult and shameless favor' he added, though an extremely important one. He said that in his family, it was tradition to offer a prayer at the exact location of a kin's passing (one's religious inclination not being relevant). Given the circumstances, however, neither him nor his wife could bring themselves to do this. He asked of me: please, it does not have to be soon; it does not have to be in the foreseeable future, even. *But please, when you get a chance, return to the island just one more time, and offer my son a prayer. It would mean the world to me.*

I promised him that I would, and entered the funeral house.

I greeted Matt's mother with a silent and solemn bow. The skin on her face hung like withered dough, exhausted from all the mourning. It seemed that in the moment she couldn't quite register who I was, which I understood completely.

Then I stood before Matt's photograph, framed in black, propped on a mahogany stand in front of his casket. There are three bows to be performed in a Korean funeral rite: two full bows, and one standard. A full bow brings the visitor close to the ground—both knees knelt and forehead touching the floor. The repetition of this bow is a form of greeting reserved for the dead: a show of utmost respect and sincerity which is undeserved—or rather, unearned as of yet—for those still left breathing on this earth (in a cosmic, philosophical sense—if I am not mistaken). And respect Matt I did, objectively as a person of good character, and subjectively as a friend who had accompanied me through some formative years of my life. Upon my first bow, I thought of our many escapades together and everyone related therein: Matt himself, JY, Mr. K, and all the other faces who have painted themselves vividly in the canvas of my remembrance. For Matt and I both, it was now truly time to let by-gone adventures be.

Then on the second bow, I remembered.

Matt's father passed away ten years ago, and I had no idea what he looked like.

About the Author

CHRISTOPHER HANN hails from New Zealand—a distant yet charming pair of islands on the far side of the globe. He is of Korean descent (a 'Kiwi-Korean', so to speak) and hasn't thought twice about his love for horror since reading 'The Black Cat' by Poe. His has short stories appearing in two anthologies, **BEYOND THE BOUNDS OF INFINITY** and **SILK & SINEW**. He is currently working on his debut novel.